B*ill*ie and the Parent Plan

I don't even care that the seat's hard. I don't care that Granny Caroline's perfume is getting up my nose from one side, and Victoria keeps whispering things in lipstick breath into my ear on the other side. There isn't any room left in my brain for thinking about those things because of concentrating so hard on the back of Mum's head.

And this is why. I'm trying to do something my best friend, Archie, told me about, called thought transference, so I can make Mum realize that this is her last chance to get out of marrying stupid old Quentin...

Just say no, Mum. You've got to. Just say no. SAY! NO!

Ann Bryant originally trained as a musician, and went on to teach music, drama and dance, as well as writing scripts, poetry, songs and stories for children's television. Although she still teaches part time, writing is now Ann's greatest passion and she is the author of many successful series, including *The Café Club*, *Step-Chain*, *Make Friends With* and *Ballerina Dreams*. *Billie and the Parent Plan* is her first full-length novel.

To find out more about Ann Bryant, visit her website: www.annbryant.co.uk

B*ill*ie and the Parent Plan

Charley
Sullivan.

Ann Bryant

USBORNE

Also by Ann Bryant

Ballerina Dreams

Poppy's Secret Wish
Jasmine's Lucky Star
Rose's Big Decision
Dancing Princess
Dancing with the Stars
Dancing For Ever

To Jody with all my love

First published in 2005 by Usborne Publishing Ltd.,
Usborne House, 83-85 Saffron Hill, London EC1N 8RT, England. www.usborne.com

Text copyright © Ann Bryant, 2005
The right of Ann Bryant to be identified as the author of this work has been asserted
by her in accordance with the Copyright, Designs and Patents Act, 1988.

The name Usborne and the devices ♀ 🎈 are Trade Marks of
Usborne Publishing Ltd.

A CIP catalogue record for this book is available from the British Library.

JFMAMJ ASOND/05
ISBN 0 7460 6755 0

Printed in Great Britain.

1 The Beginning of the End

My name's Billie Stubbs. Well, to tell the truth it's *Millie* Stubbs, but when I was four, I had a bad cold and a blocked-up nose one day, and the lady from the newspaper shop asked me what my name was. And I tried to say Millie, but it came out like *Billie.* You'll see what I mean if you block your own nose and try it. The lady said, "Oh that's a nice name! I've never heard of Billie for a girl before!" And all day long I kept trying it out and making Mum say it too, and when I woke up the next day I still liked it, so then I made everyone say it and it just kind of stuck.

This is a description of me. I'm ten years and three hundred and forty-nine days old, which makes me nearly eleven, and I'm quite small for my age with bluey-grey eyes, and straight, dark-brown hair that comes down to the end of my sleeves – when I'm wearing short sleeves, that is. Like right now. These sleeves are part of a dress that's long and tight and shiny and dark gold, and swirls out at the bottom if you whizz round. Mum and I chose it together, and for once *he* wasn't around and neither was Victoria. Of course Mum made me try it on for *him*, and he said I looked like a film star in it. How stupid is that? How can a nearly eleven-year-old look like a film star? And Victoria, my eighteen-year-old, very, very nearly stepsister, gave me one of her big squelchy kisses and said I looked good enough to eat. Pathetic! So now I'm sitting on an extremely hard seat in the Register Office staring at the back of Mum's head and feeling like a custard pie. Great!

This is a terrible day. Not because of the dress. Because of *him.*

Quentin.

I don't even care that the seat's hard. I don't care that Granny Caroline's perfume is getting up my nose from *one* side, and, Victoria keeps whispering things in lipstick breath into my ear on the *other* side. There isn't any room left in my brain for thinking about those things because of concentrating so hard on the back of Mum's head. And this is why. I'm trying to do something my best friend, Archie, told me about called thought transference, so I can make Mum realize that this is her last chance to get out of marrying stupid old Quentin. Some people don't actually mean *old* when they say *stupid old*, like "*This stupid old pen won't work.*" But *I* mean it. You see, Quentin's fifty-three, which is old enough to be a granddad, and my mum's only thirty-six.

This is your very, very last chance, Mum…

"Do you, Emma Stubbs, take Quentin Taylor Crawford to be your lawful, wedded husband…?"

Just say no, Mum. You've got to. Please don't marry that ancient old antique dinosaur! Just say no. SAY! NO!

"I do."

My whole body feels like sliding down to the floor and dissolving into nothingness. *Mum! What have you done?*

They're smiling at each other now and I'm going

frozen on the inside, thinking back to how it all began. If only she hadn't gone to that dinner party in Somerset, she would never have met Quentin in the first place. Then I wouldn't be stuck here, like the saddest, crossest person in the entire world, with the most boring, old-fashioned, *looks-like-a-granddad* man for my stepfather. I stared out of the Register Office window and went off into a daydream. If Quentin and I lived in the animal kingdom I would be a small black-and-white chimp and he would be a raggedy old grey mongoose. That's how different we are. And now my last hope has gone.

I've always gone off into thought bubbles and daydreams, and I think I was probably five when my imaginings about having a new dad started. I used to draw pictures of him at school, but they were rubbish because art is my worst thing. I can only really draw clouds and sheep. (A sheep is a cloud with four lines coming out of the bottom.)

But one day, when my mum had been to Parents' Evening the night before, she asked me if I ever wished I had a dad, same as other children. I guessed Miss Pope must have shown her the drawings of my imaginary dad, so I asked Mum if she liked them and Mum had tears in her eyes and I didn't get why because there was nothing to be sad about. Then she asked me again if I wished I had a dad and I said "a bit" because it felt as though "no" would have been too rude to say, even though it was the truth. You see, I was so little, and I couldn't explain that the reason I didn't mind about not having a dad was because I had Mum. I'd never even met my real dad, and actually he'd never met me either because he went off before I was born. The imaginary dad person was just in my thought bubbles. For fun. Mum was real life. She was the one who cuddled me and made up all the games. I can still remember those ones from when I was four. There was the *Jump out of bed* game, the *Get dressed* game, the *Eat up breakfast* game and all the other games right till the *Guess what the bedtime story will be* game.

As I got older I felt as though I was getting to know the dad in my thought bubbles better, and when I was about eight he was wearing jogging bottoms and a T-shirt and looking a bit sweaty because he'd been working out at the gym to keep fit, and then he'd come home so he could go out for a run with me because that's what we both loved doing most. I'm quite a good runner – I mean in real life, not just in my dream – and the new dad was really keen to make me even better by helping me with my training.

I've scribbled that training dream down on a scrap of paper and stuffed it in my private box in my drawer with my other scribbled thoughts and ideas and dreams. The box is full now because in the last three months, which is how long Quentin and Victoria have been living in *our* house, things have changed. I've had more thought bubbles and done more scribbling than ever before. You see, I really *do* want a new dad now. A young one, like the one in my eight-year-old thought bubble. Someone who'd come along and sweep Mum off her feet and *make her get rid of Quentin*. And I've been doing everything in my power to try and make that happen. For a start I developed a big keenness on shopping which Mum couldn't understand.

"Why do you keep wanting to go to the supermarket, Billie?"

But I could hardly tell her I was on the lookout for a man like the one in my daydreams, with spiky brown hair and jogging bottoms and a sweaty T-shirt, and the moment I saw one I planned to accidentally bump into him with the supermarket trolley, which would get Mum talking to him, and once she'd taken a proper look she'd instantly realize she'd made a big mistake choosing someone with a bald patch on top and the side bits all grey. Why did she *do* that? *Why?* I don't get her.

But now it's too late. My beautiful big thought bubbles have been popped for good, because Mum's actually gone and done the very worst thing ever and married stupid old Quentin. Well, I'm not telling people that he's my dad. I'm not even saying I've got a new stepdad. I'm not saying anything at all.

Mum's wedding dress is like a suit. It's creamy coloured and the skirt goes right down to the floor. I must admit she looks very pretty today with all her sparkly jewellery. Quentin looks boring. His suit is grey with stripes. When he turns his head in a certain way the side of his cheek gets a big fold in it. Yuk!

I suddenly realized I'd been stuck in a thought

bubble for ages, and I'd just done one of those big shivery shudders that your brain doesn't actually tell your body to do, so now Victoria's holding my hand as though I'm a baby or something.

"It's very emotional, isn't it, Billie?"

I didn't answer her. It's so annoying with Victoria because she acts like she's all wise and she knows everything about me and my feelings, partly because she's eighteen and partly because she thinks she's my sister. Well, I don't want a sister any more than I want a stepfather.

Ever since Victoria's been living in our house, she's been trying to get me to tell her my thoughts, but they're private and there's no way I'd ever tell *anyone*, so I definitely wouldn't tell *her*. The other very annoying thing that Victoria is always doing, is hugging me, and she's doing it right now because she thinks I'm emotional from this horrible wedding. Which just proves that she doesn't understand me at all.

"It makes you feel a bit teary, doesn't it, Billie?"

"No."

I'd said it under my breath but she heard.

"Listen to you, all gruff!"

Then she kissed me and I could feel the stickiness from her lipstick on my face. I was trying to rub it off without her noticing when Granny Caroline's arm went round me from the other side, and I found myself squashed into one of her massive boobs.

"Lovely, isn't it, dear?"

I couldn't answer her, partly because I couldn't really move my mouth but partly because I was too fed up to answer. You see, I'd suddenly had a pounce thought. That's one of those thoughts that crouches right down inside your brain for ages, all stinky and slimy, but you're not really aware of anything except a bad feeling hanging around in your head, and then it suddenly pounces and makes you shake with fear.

This is the thought that pounced on me...I'd heard Victoria and Mum giggling about how there would probably be a wedding photo of Mum and Quentin in the paper, and I hadn't really thought there was anything wrong with that. But now I could see something hugely, massively wrong about it, because if anyone sees the photo they'll know that Quentin is my new stepdad, and I won't be able to deny it. And there's someone in my class at school who absolutely must *not* see it. Not ever. His name's Liam. Liam Compton. If Liam saw it my life would be even worse than it is now. In fact it wouldn't be worth living.

Oh go away, pounce thought! Go away! Go away! Leave me alone!

2 The Change in Mum

The last three and a half days have been terrible. I've had to put up with Victoria kissing and cuddling me and calling me sweetie and angel, and I've also had to look at her stringy little knickers hanging in the bathroom, while Mum and Quentin have been away on what they call a mini honeymoon. But now they're back things are even worse. You see, they've been learning ballroom dancing, and they just can't stop doing it in the kitchen and the sitting room and even on the landing. They push the furniture back and put their old-fashioned music on and stand with their chins tipped in a funny way, wearing stupid smiles on their faces. Then off they go with their arms sticking out, doing sharp turns and sudden clasps and all the time counting under their breath. They obviously think they look good, but actually it's just totally embarrassing.

I've been moaning like mad to Archie Griggs, my best friend in the world. Archie and I have known each other since nursery school. It's hard to explain to people why I like him so much. It's probably partly because we've always been together so we're really used to each other, but it's also partly because I don't have to pretend anything with Archie – like pretend I fancy boys, or pretend to care about my hair or my clothes. That doesn't mean that I prefer all boys to all girls because I don't. Archie's an example of a nice boy, that's all.

I told him how awful the wedding was and how the worst bit was the reception because Mum and Quentin made yucky speeches about finding each other, and they kept on going on about families, and I wished I could block my ears because I hated listening to Mum making out that Victoria and Quentin belong in our family when they don't. Mum's such a traitor.

"It's terrible round here," I moaned to Archie when he phoned on Saturday morning.

"So just ignore it till it gets better," was all Archie said. Then he started on about his latest computer game.

"It's brilliant, Billie! You can see it when you come for lunch."

"Am I coming for lunch?"

"Yeah, Mum's going to ask your mum in a minute. That's what I was phoning about."

I was really pleased because I love going to Archie's house, and these days I love it even more because it feels like a proper home with nice *young* people in it.

"Has your mum bought the local paper this week, Arch?"

"Dunno. Why?"

"Because my mum has, and there's a big close-up wedding photo of her and Quentin in it."

"Oh right."

"Don't you get it, Arch? Liam might see it and if he does he'll start on me on Monday, and then they'll all be at it – the whole gang."

"Pretend you don't care. Then he'll get bored and stop bothering."

"But what about…"

I so nearly told him the awful thing that had happened in town the other day, which was the *real* reason I didn't want Liam to realize that Mum and Quentin were married, but I couldn't talk about that yet. Maybe I'd tell him when I went over for lunch. Yes, that would be better. I had to tell *someone*. It was too scary to keep to myself.

"What about *what*?"

"Nothing."

"Get your mum then, Billie, and I'll get mine."

So that's what we did and while Mum was talking to Archie's mum, she was waving an envelope at me and making big eyes, which meant *Don't go away because I want you to post this letter for me.*

The postbox is a hundred and fifty-two and a half metres away. I know that because Archie once measured it with a tape measure. We were bored in the holidays, and I said let's have a day of guessing all different things and we'll see who gets the most right answers. I guessed that the postbox would be forty-seven metres away so I lost that one. But then we had a race to it, and I won easily because of running being my best thing.

Once when I was in Year One and I won the fifty metres heat, Mum told me that I might have got my running skills from my dad because he used to be a fast runner. I remember asking Mum if he was coming to watch me at Sports Day and Mum squeezing my hand tight and saying he'd gone to another country now, so he wouldn't be able to come because it was a bit too far. And I asked her if he was ever coming back, and she said no in a sad voice. I'd only asked her because I didn't want him turning up out of the blue and spoiling our lovely two-people family. But now I wish I'd tried to explain how I felt, then Mum might have thought a bit more carefully before she got married again. Especially to an *old man*.

I was deep in a thought bubble about running in the Olympic Games when Mum put the phone down and handed me the letter to post. I was thinking that it might truly be possible for me to run in the Olympic Games one day if I really trained hard. You see I've got better and better at running since

Year One, and once I did actually represent the school. And that gave me an idea.

"Can you time me running there and back, Mum?"

But she must have suddenly remembered something. "Oh whoops! Out of the way, Billie!" She pushed past me and raced into the kitchen. "I left the potatoes. They'll be boiling away…"

I followed her into the kitchen and saw her accidentally knock a pot of jam off the worktop when she was lunging at the cooker to turn off the gas. Little red globules spattered all over the floor, and Mum huffed and puffed as she bent down to wipe them up.

"Ugh! I'll never get rid of all this stickiness," she said as she wrung the cloth out.

But I'd got the idea about running and training in my head now and I couldn't leave it alone. "*Can* you, Mum?"

"What?"

"Time me."

I could tell she wasn't paying proper attention because she just said, "Get ready, set, go!"

"But I'm not ready…let me get to the front door first. And you haven't even looked at your watch."

"Hurry up then. I'm trying to make…" I saw that her cheeks had gone a bit red. Then her voice went all gooey. "Well, actually it's the anniversary of the day Quentin and I first met each other so I wanted to make it an extra-special meal. It's hotpot. That's his favourite!" She giggled. "He doesn't know I'm making it. He's just popped out to get some wine, you see."

Why was she telling me all this? Did she think I was interested? I didn't care if Quentin had just popped out to Mars to get a Mars Bar. All I wanted was for Mum to time me running to the postbox. And now I was mad because she'd gone back to her wiping and forgotten all about me.

It was Quentin's fault. Everything was Quentin's fault. If Mum had spilled loads of jam all over the floor before *he* lived here, she probably would have made a game out of it. I could just imagine her looking at all the little globules through half-closed eyes to see if they happened to have landed in the shape of an animal or anything. And then it would have been my turn to look for a shape. You see Mum's imagination is just as big as mine. At least it used to be. Now she's more interested in Quentin than in me, she doesn't invent good games any more. Well she did once, only *he* tried to join in and it didn't work because he hasn't got any imagination at all. So he just kept grinning at me and saying, "Good fun, Billie, isn't it?" and things like that. And I said, "No," under my breath.

It's funny, but now I've started noticing so much stuff about Quentin, it's made me notice Mum more too, and compare her with other mothers, like Archie's mum, Suky. If I had Suky for a mum I'd be really proud because she looks like a model. It must be great having a model-looking mother.

I was watching Mum scouring away at the last little patch of jammy floor. It was surprising how many bits of her wobbled when she did that. Suky wouldn't have wobbled. I think it was that thought that completely put me out of the mood for running. I didn't even say bye to Mum when I went out of the back door. She wouldn't have heard me anyway because she was singing in a warbly voice a song that went, "Did you ever know that you're my hero?"

Yuk. Yuk. Yuk.

Going round the side of the house to the front gate my heart started to beat a bit faster and my footsteps slowed down. I didn't open the gate straight away. There was something I had to do first. I've always done it – well since Year Five, anyway, but it's especially important these days. I stood on the great big plant pot just inside the gate. From up there I can see all the way down the road and some of the way up too. If anyone was walking along or just hanging around I'd see them before they saw me.

Look right, look left, look right again. And just one more check to the left. Phew!

No Liam.

3 The Bullying

As I walked along I kept turning round to check that Liam wasn't creeping up behind me. It's horrible having to worry about someone all the time, but I do have to, because he used to hang about my house loads when he was bullying me about Archie being my boyfriend in Year Five. His mum lets him go off on his own whenever he wants, you see, and she doesn't check up on him or anything, and I just know he's going to turn up again one of these days because of the thing that happened last week – the real reason why I don't want him to see the wedding photo of Mum and Quentin in the paper.

It was last Monday when it happened. Liam came up to me in the playground with a big sneer all over his face, which made my heart beat faster straight away.

"Tom saw your mum in town, holding hands with a man. How come she's got such an *old* boyfriend?"

His lip was curling when he said the last two words, as if having anything to do with old people makes you come out in infectious spots. So I had to make something up quickly so it wouldn't turn out to be like Year Five with all the horrible bullying going on. I suddenly thought of something inspirational (to use my teacher's favourite word, which is also mine now) and said it was my granddad, and that he was only holding Mum's hand because she'd just been attacked by a gang of muggers and was a bit shaky from fighting them off.

I remember feeling lovely and clever for about two seconds because Liam looked quite impressed, but then my cleverness melted away when I heard his mean voice come back.

"What, so your granddad lives with you or something?"

The inside of my head went mad with thoughts crashing around about how to answer him. The first thought was: *Do what Archie does, Billie. Pretend you don't care. Just say "So what if he does live with us? What's it to you?"* But that thought got squeezed into nothingness because the whole gang were standing round Liam by then, and they'd all got smirky lips.

"He's just visiting us, okay?" I wrinkled my nose and gave him a big *doh* look, even though my heart was beating madly, but he just kept staring as though I hadn't even spoken, so then I tried to think of something else to say to make it sound more interesting.

"He lives in Australia, you see…"

"Whoa!" said Liam, turning round to his friends and putting on an Australian accent. "Aus-try-lia, ay?"

I could feel myself starting to go red because instead of making things better, I'd made them worse. I already had to make sure no one saw Mum and Quentin holding hands again, but now I'd got to make sure no one heard Quentin speak either. I'd have to work out a plan for that later. Right now all I wanted was to think of something really cool about

Quentin that might impress Liam enough to make him stop staring like that, so I sent my mind flick-flick-flicking through all the things that Quentin does.

He works in an office.

He sits in an armchair.

He reads.

Boring.

He sits at his desk.

He writes letters.

He helps Mum.

Boring, boring, boring.

He washes the car.

He mows the lawn.

He hums.

He talks to Mum and Victoria.

He reads magazines.

He reads magazines! Yes, brilliant!

A picture of a big bright gleaming motorbike came flashing into my head. I'd seen it on the front cover of a magazine that's always on the kitchen table these days. If Quentin wasn't so old he'd be able to actually ride a motorbike instead of just reading about them all the time. But at least it had given me an idea. I could remember the name of the motorbike easily because I'd seen the picture so often. And before I knew it, I'd blurted out, "It's quite good actually, because Quen…Granddad's got a Honda Goldwing and he takes me for rides on it."

There was a silence like a finger snap after those words of mine, and I saw a little sparkle come into Liam's eyes. And just for that tiny amount of time I really thought everything was going to be okay after all. But then his whole gang cracked up and fell about laughing, and a massive sneer came over Liam's face.

"Yeah? So how did he get it over from Australia then?"

I haven't got the kind of brain that can work out facts. It only seems to do dreams and imaginings, but I tried to think what Archie would say. And then I got it.

"On a ship!" My mouth was going dry because of what Liam might say next, and I wished I dared to tell him to go away (in swear words).

"You'll have to show me that *mean machine* then, Billie, won't you!"

Those were the last words he'd said to me and I can still hear the hardness in his voice. It's making my legs feel a bit shaky as I'm turning into Derwent Road where the postbox is.

Then the hairs on my arms stood up and my eyes felt as though they were going to pop out of my head because there he was, down at the end of the road. Liam. Kicking something around with Isaac, Josh and Tom watching him and laughing.

Quick as a flash I pressed myself into the hedge before he saw me. I hadn't realized how prickly it would be though, so when a rough twig scraped my cheek and poked my eye I had to jump out again. Then there was nothing else for it but to run back the way I'd come with my eye throbbing like mad and my brain going off into horrible scary thought bubbles… *What if Liam comes right up to my house and Quentin's just coming back with the wine? What if Tom says, "Hello, you're Billie's granddad, aren't you?" And the worst "What if…" What if Liam asks him if he can have a look at his Honda Goldwing?*

My knees were trembling so much by then that I could hardly run, especially with one eye closed. It was such a massive relief to get to the back door that I sort of flopped into it and landed in a heap on the kitchen floor.

"Billie!" Mum's voice was a mixture of surprised and cross. "What's the matter? Where have you been?" She was staring at the letter that I was still clutching. I'd forgotten about that.

I got up slowly to give myself time to think and saw that she was peering at me with a worried frown. "What happened to your eye?"

"Erm…I was…looking in a hedge at a bird's nest, you see…and a twig poked me right in the eye."

"Oh dear, that must have hurt…"

She held my chin and turned my face to the side as she peered into my eye.

"And I couldn't see anything and I thought I might have actually blinded myself so I came home."

She kissed me then and did a little chuckle. "You do get yourself into some scrapes, don't you, love?"

But then Victoria walked in, all bright-eyed and excited, and Mum forgot about me straight away.

"We-ell?" she said in a stupid slow voice. It was

as though she and Victoria had got a big secret together. "Let's have a look!"

And Victoria opened the bag she was carrying with a big flourish and said, "I bought the blue one!"

The blue thing that she was holding up looked hideous, like a swimsuit, only floaty and lacy, so it obviously wasn't for swimming in.

"It's lovely, Tigs!"

I hate it when Mum calls her that. She's just copying Quentin, but he's known Victoria for miles longer than Mum has. I went stomping off upstairs because they both got on my nerves so much, and Mum must have remembered my eye then because she said, "Oh Tigs, could you be a gem and sort Billie out while I set the table? She poked a twig in her eye by mistake."

"Poor sweetie!" said Victoria catching up with me. She tried to put her arm round me, but I wriggled out of it and asked her what time it was. I couldn't wait to get to Archie's now, where no one's old and no one's posh and no one's gooey and giggly.

As Victoria dabbed away with some stingy smelly stuff, I went off into a thought bubble imagining that

Mum and Quentin had gone on a really long honeymoon that lasted about two months, and Archie's mum had invited me to stay with them for the whole time. It was great thinking those thoughts apart from Victoria spoiling them by talking all through.

"How ever did you do this, Billie?" Her eyes were so close to my face that I could see the little bobbles of mascara on her eyelashes.

"Looking at a nest."

"You're a right one, aren't you?"

I didn't answer. I wanted to get back to my thoughts.

"I'll pop you over to Archie's so your mum and my dad can have a few special moments to themselves, all right?" She giggled.

Huh! I nearly pointed out that it was about time Mum and *I* had a few special moments together, because every single moment used to be precious before two certain people turned up and spoiled everything. But I just kept those thoughts inside me, where they boiled and bubbled madly.

"All right, sweetie?" Victoria asked me again, as I hadn't answered.

I nodded because I didn't feel like speaking, but the nod made a bit of the stingy stuff go on to my actual eyeball and that hurt more than when I first got the twig poked in it.

"Oh, sorry, darling! My fault entirely!" And she started giving me little goldfish kisses all over my face. "Let's wash it out with warm water…"

But I just grabbed the nearest flannel and did it myself. And right in the middle of that, just to make my day…

"Oh, there's Daddy!"

I was already in a bad enough mood but when she said that, a totally ferocious one started rising up from my feet. I'd heard the front door click too, but my temper wasn't just because of Quentin coming home, it was because of the way she called him *Daddy*. It was so babyish and made her sound extra posh. I knew what was going to happen now too. I went through it in my head in a blah blah blah voice. *Quentin will go in to see Mum in the kitchen. Mum will tell him about my eye. Quentin will come up to look at it, then he'll peer up close and say, What a corker! or one of his other stupid old-fashioned phrases.*

I wasn't going to let any of that happen so I chucked the flannel down and ran out on to the landing. And that's when I heard it. The dreaded humming. He was always doing it. Why didn't he whistle, like fathers I've seen on films? I've never heard Archie's dad humming. He's way too cool.

Quentin was looking up at me from the hall. "Had a bit of bother with a hedge, Billie?"

And that made me even madder because I couldn't help thinking about Archie's dad again. Neil wouldn't say something as stupid as that in a million years because he's not old like Quentin, that's why. I bet Quentin's old enough to be Archie's dad's *dad*.

Now I was noticing all the bad things – like the creases down the front of his trousers. Why can't he wear jeans like other dads do? And then a whole load of other "Whys" went tumbling round in my thought bubble. *Why can't he tell me off when I do stuff like break the clothes line trying to swing on it? Why does he leave all the telling off to Mum? Why doesn't he shout "Referee!" at the telly when he's watching football matches, like Neil does?*

In fact, why doesn't he watch *any football matches in the first place?*

Then right in the middle of all those *Why* questions going on inside the bubble, one suddenly came out into the open.

"Why don't you and Mum go away on another honeymoon?"

I'd given myself quite a shock saying it, but I think I must have given Quentin an even bigger one. His eyes went all confused and his cheeks seemed to hang a bit looser than usual and he took a step back. "Well…we only had the one…a short one…so that…"

Then Victoria interrupted him as she went downstairs, and I noticed her voice was all gentle.

"I'm just taking Billie over to Archie's, Daddy."

"Yes, yes, right. I'll er…see you *later*…" He suddenly grinned up at me and winked. "…*alligator!*"

"In a while, crocodile!" Victoria said. (I guess she knew *I* wasn't going to reply.) They were both grinning like mad. Anyone'd think they'd invented that rhyme or something!

Then Quentin turned serious. "Drive carefully now, Tigs."

"Don't worry, Daddy."

She smiled and patted him on the cheek, and I felt like I'd got a mouth full of *Tiggsy, Daddy, patty* stuff, and I really urgently needed to spit it out. Thank goodness for Archie and his nice normal family.

4 The Fireball

I know why Archie is *my* best friend. But sometimes I wonder why he could possibly want me to be *his* best friend.

When we were all in Year Four Archie got bullied about having to wear glasses, but it soon wore off once everyone got used to them. In Year Five he got bullied about me being his girlfriend, but he didn't seem to notice really, and that's when Liam changed his target from Archie to me, and it's also when I realized something important. It wasn't that Archie didn't *notice* the bullying, it was that he really didn't care about it. And that's the reason why Liam got fed up of bothering with Archie and swapped over to me. I pretended like mad that I couldn't care less, out it didn't work, because I'm a person who shows what I'm thinking on my face – at least that's what Mum used to say when I was little. It's true that she's not said it recently, but then we don't talk about things like that now.

I was thinking about all this while Archie was trying to get me interested in his CD-ROM before lunch.

"Look, Billie. Endangered species. It's on two CDs. I'm saving up for the second one." A picture of an orang-utan came on the screen. "See, it tells you all about them."

"Yes, but, Archie, can I just tell *you* something?"

Archie must have thought it was going to be something exciting because when I started telling him, in a bit of an embarrassed way, about how I'd seen Liam and the others near my house, he looked disappointed and said, "I've told you, Billie, just ignore them."

"You see, the problem is…" And then I told him what I'd said to Liam about Quentin being my granddad. I finished up by saying, "And if he sees the photo in the paper he'll find out I was lying, Archie. It'll be terrible. I'm dreading Monday morning!"

"Why? Just tell him you're entitled to lie if you want to lie because it's a free world."

"What! I couldn't say that! I wouldn't dare! He'd kill me!"

"Well don't say anything then. It's got nothing to do with Liam. He's not your mum, and he's not God."

Most people think that Archie's the least cool person in Year Six because he wears glasses and he always looks neat and tidy and he's got a big brain and he's quite clumsy and not much good at sport and his best friend's a girl. But I think that if they heard him say stuff like that, they'd soon realize that actually he's the coolest of them all.

A few minutes later Suky called us down for lunch. The Griggses' kitchen has got an archway in the middle. It's like a proper kitchen at one end and a dining room at the other. Archie's mum and dad don't say dining room, though, they say "dining area", which sounds all right when you're grown up, but Archie calls it that too, even though I've told him it's rather posh. And once, when we were in Year

Three and it was news time, he said it in front of the whole class. Everyone was sniggering behind their hands but as usual, Archie didn't care. He just kept right on with his news.

I was watching Archie's mum, Suky, while we helped her lay the table. I'd like to look like Suky when I grow up. She's my role model. She's tall and thin with a straight back, and wears things like jeans and cool tops and hardly any make-up. I don't think she'd ever have bobbles on *her* mascara, not like Victoria. Her hair is short and scrunchy with shiny bits. Archie's dad is also my role model because I like the way he keeps fit and looks young and tells jokes. Maisie, Archie's three-year-old sister is definitely *not* my role model, because…well, right now, for example, she's sitting on a cushion trying to scratch something off the table with her nail. She's got her tongue sticking out because of concentrating so hard, and her nose is running a bit. She is sweet, though.

I've often been to Archie's at weekends, and I always like mealtimes because Suky and Neil chat and tell funny stories, and Maisie's funny without even trying to be, and sometimes Archie and I have private jokes. But today it was specially nice to be here with two such young parents and a sweet little sister, instead of a granddad person and a posh, much older sister, who still says "Daddy".

Neil was the last one to arrive. He'd been in town having his hair cut. Before Suky sat down she pretended to be massaging his head with strong fingers. "Very trendy, Neil! Feels like a loo brush!"

"Get off," Neil said, but he was grinning.

It's good when Suky and Neil take the mickey out of each other. Mum and Quentin would never do that because they're too busy staring into each other's eyes, and anyway Quentin's too old and boring for jokes. I bet he's never played a joke in his whole life. He's probably never actually told one either, and even if he heard someone else telling one I bet he wouldn't laugh out loud. He'd just do this sort of sniffy breathing that he does from his nostrils.

It was spoiling my nice time with Archie's family, thinking about Quentin, so I went back to looking at Neil's spiky haircut, and suddenly it reminded me of the photo that Mum's got of my own dad. She's only got this one and she keeps it in the cupboard with the albums, loose, though, not stuck in. In the picture my dad is smiling, leaning against a wall, and he's got spiky hair and a little beard. Neil hasn't got a beard but his smile is a bit the same, and I started wondering what it would be like if Neil was my dad. It felt nice having that thought, only I went red because I realized I'd been staring at Neil for ages, and he was giving me a funny look as though I was mad.

"What do *you* think, Billie?"

"Er...what?" I didn't know what he was talking about because of being in the thought bubble.

"What do you reckon to my new haircut?"

"Oh...I like it!"

"Thank you, Billie. You see, some people round here appreciate a good haircut when they see one, Suke!"

"*I* do!" Maisie suddenly piped up. "I pee-chate it, Daddy!"

We all laughed. She looked really cute with hardly more than her head showing over the table.

"Stilton and leek pie, Billie?" Suky said, loading it on my plate. She knows about my big appetite.

"Thank you."

"Help yourself to new potatoes and peas."

And then the phone rang.

"I'll get it," said Neil, hurrying over to the place near the kettle, where they keep their phone.

"Hey, Rob! How yer doing, mate!" He was leaning on the worktop and grinning.

Quentin would never say "hey" or "mate" or lean on something like that. He wouldn't wear a T-shirt hanging out of his jeans either. The only thing that was the same about Quentin and Neil was their really short hair, only Quentin was half bald and the half that wasn't bald was grey. Neil's hair was a sort of...medium brown colour like mine. And he'd got brown eyes like mine too. In fact come to think about it *I* looked more like Archie's dad than Archie did. If anyone came in this room now and had to guess which one was the guest, I reckon they'd guess Archie, because his hair's almost blonde.

"Cheers, mate," said Neil, putting the phone down.

He came back to the table and started tucking into his food but my plate was nearly empty by then.

"Any more yummy pie, folks?" asked Suky, looking at me.

"Yes please!"

And Maisie pointed at me and grinned. "You're the *guest*!" I think she must have only just learnt that word, the way she said it all proudly. Archie's so lucky having a three-year-old sister instead of an eighteen-year-old who thinks she knows everything.

"Well actually, Billie's practically one of the family, Maisie."

And those words flashed into my brain like a fireball roaring out of the sky, and made the hairs on my arms stand up. I mean, Suky just said I was practically one of the family, and Archie and I are like brother and sister. So I'd fit perfectly into this family, wouldn't I? I'd be able to help look after Maisie and take Gorky, their dog, for walks and help Suky and Neil. It would be so cool.

And Mum'd be okay. It wouldn't be like I was never going to see her again. In fact she'd still be my mother and we'd see each other whenever we wanted, it was just that I wouldn't actually be living in that family with her. Anyway, Quentin and Victoria weren't really anything to do with me, were they? And they'd all have a much better time without me. They'd just be three grown-ups together, with lots of giggling and dancing and chuckling about stupid old-fashioned things. And I'd be here. In a proper young family with a lovely brother and a sweet little sister and the coolest parents in the world.

Adopted.

Yessssss!

Wicked!

5 The Start
of the Plan

"**W**hat's for pudding, Mum?" Archie asked.

"Strawberries and ice cream."

Normally the thought of strawberries and ice cream would make me really excited, but at that moment I was already totally full up to the top of my head with excitement, so there wasn't room for even a millimetre more. My whole body was buzzing with happiness and hopefulness, and my brain was trying to think what to do to make the adoption happen.

A plan. That's what I needed. Not just dreams, or ideas or thoughts in a bubble. But a proper parent plan. But how was it going to work? How was I going to get Suky and Neil to adopt me?

"Who'd like to finish off this last potato?" asked Suky. "What about you, Billie?"

I shook my head and said, "No, thank you, Suky," and realized at that precise moment that the plan had already started to form itself because I'd been so polite just then. You see, I had to make Suky and Neil really really like me and that meant being polite and generous and truthful and kind and well behaved. It would also be good if I had a talent to impress them with. Running. Yes, that was it. Well, that was actually my *only* talent, but it was the perfect one because Archie's no good at all at any kind of sport, so it would be nice for Suky and Neil to have a daughter who was a good runner.

But first things first...politeness...

"That was such a delicious first course, Suky," I said with a big smile, "that I'm completely full up. But I absolutely loved it. Especially the pie."

"Marks and Spencer's best, Billie!"

She laughed and so did Neil, then they gave each other a look. I think they might have been appreciating my good manners, and it didn't really matter that Suky hadn't actually made the pie herself.

Just because Mum wastes her time making hotpots and things, it doesn't mean everyone does. It's much more sensible buying your food and putting it in the oven. That's definitely what I'm going to do when I'm a grown-up.

"But the potatoes and peas were lovely too."

"Thank you, Billie."

I saw her exchange another look with Neil. They were definitely noticing my politeness. The plan was working.

"Right, let's get these dishes cleared away," Suky suddenly said.

And before you could say *adoption* I'd jumped out of my chair and grabbed my plate.

"It's all right, Billie," smiled Suky. "You can entertain Maisie. We'll manage this lot." She picked up a couple of dishes.

"You're the guest," repeated Maisie with a grin.

I grinned back. She wouldn't be saying that soon. She'd be saying, "You're my sister!"

Archie sighed and took his plate out to the utility room where the dishwasher is.

"Take more than one at a time, Archie!" said Neil.

"I'll load the dishwasher, then we'll be all tidy by the time the strawberries and ice cream are on the table."

When Archie came back for the rest of the plates I asked him if I could have some more Coke.

"Yeah, course. But don't let Maisie have any. She's not allowed." Then out he went really slowly so he wouldn't drop anything.

Poor Maisie. Why wasn't she allowed any more? It didn't seem very fair. Archie probably wanted it all for himself. He's Coke mad. Maybe I'd pour a nice big beakerful for Maisie. After all it was very important for my adoption plan that *everyone* in the family liked me a lot.

"Would you like some more, Maise?" I asked with a big sisterly smile.

Her eyes grew round. "Am I allowed?"

"Course you are," I told her with another smile. "We don't listen to your silly brother, Archie, do we?"

She shook her head, looking solemn, then I filled her beaker almost to the brim and she stared at the brown fizz with big excited eyes as though it was the tooth fairy or Father Christmas. I held the beaker for her while she drank the first bit, so it didn't spill, but then she grabbed it from me with two hands and started gulping the Coke down like her life depended on it. She drank the whole lot all in one, put the beaker down and did a little burp.

"Here we are," said Suky, coming back a second later. "I'll just get the strawberries. Back in a mo."

"More?" asked Maisie as soon as we were on our own again. She was looking at me with those big eyes.

"Okay, but don't drink it so quickly this time, all right?"

She nodded and just took a few gulps then put her beaker down as Neil and Suky and Archie all came back together.

Neil was rubbing his hands and licking his lips at the sight of the strawberries. "Mmm! Lovely!" he said. "Nice big juicy ones!"

"Hey, where's all the Coke gone?" said Archie. "Have you drunk all that, Billie?"

"Maisy-Daisy drunk some too!" Maisie said, sticking her chin out at Archie.

"You better not have done, young lady!" said Suky. "You know you're not allowed!"

My heart was starting to beat a bit faster.

"I…I only gave her a little bit…" I said in a small voice. "I had all the rest of it."

"I told you Maisie wasn't allowed," said Archie.

"I know… That's why I only gave her a little bit…"

"That's okay, Billie. Don't look so worried," smiled Neil. He was such a nice, understanding father. "She's allergic to Coke, you see – if she drinks too much of it. But she'll be fine if you only gave her a bit."

Suky peered into Maisie's beaker. "Yes, she's still got quite a bit left. But this is her second glass, so don't drink it all, Maisie, all right?

Now my heart really was beating fast. I looked at Maisie and prayed she wouldn't say it was actually her third glass. She didn't have a rash or anything, thank goodness. But maybe it took a bit longer to come out.

"It makes her go a bit wild," explained Suky.

Uh-oh…

"More than wild!" said Archie, grinning round at everyone. "She goes completely hyper and shouts out rude things and does weird dancing."

"Okay, that's enough, thank you very much, Archie!" said Suky, giving Archie a stern look.

"Oh Mu-um, can't I just tell Billie about that time when you went to pick Maisie up from that party?"

I was beginning to feel a bit sick.

Suky put on a teacher's face. "Just so long as we all remember that Maisie's a very polite little girl really," she said, looking carefully at Maisie to make sure she was listening properly. "It's only Coke that makes you silly, isn't it, love?"

Maisie nodded, but she was grinning, and I noticed that while Archie was talking she was pulling funny faces.

"You see, Mum picked her up from Alice Grey's party and found Maisie dancing round the room shouting, 'Big pooh, bottom, bum!' And afterwards we found out that that's what Coke does to some kids because of the additives, so Mum made the rule that Maisie's only allowed a little drink once a week as a treat."

I tried to make my face look as though I appreciated Archie's story but also thought it was a serious matter. The trouble was my heart was sinking down to my socks at the thought of what I'd done.

"Anyway, there's nothing to worry about," said Suky.

She was smiling at me and I tried to smile back, but it was probably too wobbly to come out as a smile. Suky had no idea that there was actually *plenty* to worry about because I'd already messed up the adoption plan and it was still only brand new.

Maisie had stopped nodding now, but she was wriggling round in her chair and doing little giggles.

"So you're quite sure you only gave her a bit, Billie?" asked Neil, frowning at me.

I gulped. I couldn't tell the truth. Not now. It was too late. It would make two bad things that I'd done. One was ignoring Archie when he told me that Maisie wasn't allowed any more Coke, and the other was lying about how much I'd given her. So I nodded and prayed that Maisie would keep quiet. I could hardly swallow my ice cream, I was so busy watching her out of the corner of my eye. No one else was paying any attention to her by then because they were all concentrating on eating up their strawberries and ice cream, but Maisie was puffing her cheeks in and out and rolling her eyes round and round.

Suky's serving spoon was hovering over the strawberry bowl. "Few more then, Billie?"

I was just about to say no thank you, *you* have the last few, Suky, when Maisie opened her mouth and did a massive burp.

"Excuse *me*!" said Suky.

"I beg your *pardon*!" said Neil.

Archie cracked up.

I very nearly did too, but I managed to stop myself just in time.

"It's not funny," said Neil, frowning hard.

I'd never seen him looking stern, and it gave me a bit of a shock. Thank goodness I'd kept my laughter inside.

"What do you say, Maisie?" said Suky.

"'Scoose me."

Now Suky was looking a bit stern too and my heart was thumping away. I had to get her attention away from Maisie, but my voice seemed to have grown a bit of a stutter.

"L-lovely ice cr-cream, S-Suky."

She gave me a sort of half smile, then looked back at Maisie, who was making herself go cross-eyed and sucking her cheeks in.

"Don't be silly, Maisie," said Neil. "You're just showing off."

Archie was having a real problem stopping himself from laughing at Maisie's funny face, but I wasn't going to laugh. No way. Suky and Neil would soon see that I was taking this seriously, like them.

"What have you two got planned for this afternoon?" asked Suky. I think she was trying to stop us all looking at Maisie so she wouldn't carry on showing off.

Archie's shoulders were shaking with trapped laughter still, so it was up to me to answer.

"We're not really sure," I said in my most sensible, grown-up voice. Then I had a brainwave. "Is there anything we could do to help you?"

Suky's eyes widened. "Not unless you want to give Maisie's hair a trim," she answered. I was about to say I'd certainly love to, when she said, "Only joking!" then turned to Maisie. "It's a haircut day today, isn't it, hmm?"

Maisie giggled. A big fat giggle.

"Uh-oh!" said Suky. "It looks like—"

But she didn't get any further because Maisie cleared her throat loudly, stuck her chin in the air and began singing at the top of her voice.

"Oh the grand old Duke of York
He was a grand old dork..."

Everyone burst out laughing, even Neil, and I breathed a sigh of big relief. I should have known that good old Neil and Suky would see the funny side of it. Mum would have done too. But Quentin wouldn't. He'd probably say that *dork* was rude. In fact he probably hadn't even *heard* of the word.

Maisie grinned round the table at everyone, then opened her mouth again and stretched up her neck so her voice came out a bit strangled.

"He marched his soldiers up the hill
And then he made his drink all spill.
Pow!"

And as she sang that last bit, she took a big swipe at her beaker so it went hurtling off the table, a great stream of Coke flying out of it. Splat! It went everywhere. Then she put her finger on her lips in a funny, really grown-up way, said, "Whoops!" and slid out of her chair down to the floor.

A big snort of laughter came out of me by mistake. I straight away wished I could shove it back inside, though, because no one else was laughing now. I clapped my hand over my mouth just as Neil made the table jump – he'd got up so fast to pick up Maisie's beaker.

"Oh my God! She's gone completely mad!" said Suky, diving to the sink for a cloth.

Maisie was under the table still singing like nothing had happened. *"Oh the grand old Duke of strawberries..."* Then she suddenly popped up, put her hands on her waist and broke into a sideways gallop. "Yahoy!" she yelled out.

Gorky, who'd been in his basket in the utility room until now, came in to see what was going on. He stood there wagging his tail and panting a bit, just as Maisie came careering round the table. Of course, she bashed straight into him and toppled over, giggling like mad and kicking her legs in the air. Gorky must have smelt some Coke on the floor because he began to snuffle at the carpet with strange growly noises.

Archie was creased up in one of those silent laughs that hurts your stomach, but no way did *I* feel like laughing because Suky and Neil were both looking deadly serious. I bet they were thinking that this was all my fault. In fact they were probably thinking it was all my fault *and* I was a big liar. If only I could make time go backwards and start the parent plan all over again from when Archie and Neil cleared away the first course.

"Right, that's enough now!" said Suky, bending down to pick Maisie up.

Neil grabbed Gorky and lugged him off into the utility room. When he came back to the table and sat down, Maisie was just saying, "Silly Billie gave me lots and lots, didn't you?" She was sitting on her mum's lap sucking her thumb. A big scary silence came after those words, and I didn't know what to say so I just whispered, "Sorry, I didn't realize..."

"It's all right, Billie," said Suky. "You'll know another time, won't you?" She was smiling but only just, and I could tell she was annoyed.

It seemed like I'd been in a bright silky gold thought bubble for a short time when I'd had my inspirational idea, but now the bubble had popped and the gold was trickling away.

"It looks as if madam here is calming down, thank goodness!" said Neil.

Maisie kept her thumb in her mouth and started humming loudly when he said that.

"Can we get down, Mum?" said Archie. "I want to show Billie my CD-ROM. We didn't have time before."

I couldn't believe it. Archie was acting completely normally, as though nothing much had happened. But I suppose nothing much *had* happened as far as he was concerned. He didn't know about the parent plan.

"All right, off you go then, you two," said Suky brightly. Then she turned to Neil. "Fancy a coffee?"

"Yeah, that'd be nice."

So now everyone was back to normal! Phew! I must be the luckiest girl on the planet. I nearly started skipping, I was so happy as I followed Archie out of the room. That had been one narrow escape, but from now on I was going to be on my very best behaviour and nothing was going to get in the way of my plan.

Nothing.

6 The "Trim" Part of the Plan

It was as Archie and I were on our way upstairs to his room that I had a brilliant brainwave about how to make a really good impression on Suky. I knew I had to think about Neil too but I'd come back to that later. The only question was, should I tell Archie about my plan? I don't mean my brainwave, I mean the whole big parent plan. What would he say?

If I told him and he said it wouldn't work, I'd feel terrible. And I know Archie. He always thinks about things in a sensible way. He'd be sure to say that you can't just get adopted by another family because of the law or something. So I decided it would be better to keep quiet until I'd managed to make it a bit more definite.

All the same, he'd wonder why I wanted to help Suky all of a sudden, so I had to say something…

"Hey, Arch," I began in an excited voice as we shut his bedroom door behind us, "why don't we give your mum a nice surprise and cut Maisie's hair ourselves to save her from having to go into town?"

He was looking at me as though I'd suggested selling Maisie. "But we don't know how to cut hair…"

"*You* might not, but *I* do," I told him, trying to make my voice a bit mysterious.

"How come?"

"Because…Victoria taught me."

He sucked in his lips, which is what he does when he's not sure about something. "She's supposed to be having a trim. Trims are when you do it really neatly, you know."

"Trims are the easiest, actually."

But his lips hadn't gone back out again yet and that meant he was still thinking about it.

"Go on, Arch. It'll really help your mum."

"Why are you wanting to help Mum, all of a sudden?" His eyes were so narrow they were practically closed. "What are you up to, Billie?"

I nearly told him then. But he might think it was stupid. And what if he said he didn't want me as a sister and he'd rather we just stayed best friends? I didn't want to think about that.

"It's only that I'm feeling kind of guilty because of it being my fault that Maisie went hyper."

"Yeah, but you didn't know, did you? You don't have to worry about that, Billie. Mum and Dad aren't mad or anything."

"I know, but I'd still like to try and make up for it…"

He was frowning a bit. I think he was trying to understand how I felt. "Okay." He opened his bedroom window and leaned out.

I could see Neil sitting on the grass making a daisy chain. Maisie was skipping round the lawn singing *"Daisy, Daisy, give me your Auntie Sue."* I think her playgroup must do a lot of songs.

"We'll look after Maisie for a bit, if you want, Dad," Archie called out.

Neil shielded his eyes from the sun and looked up at us, surprised.

"Yeah…great!"

This would be a good chance to impress Neil.

"Say it was my idea," I hissed into the back of Archie's neck, but Archie can't have heard me because he just said, "That's all right," and shut the window.

A few minutes later when Maisie came up to Archie's room, I clapped her hands together inside my hands because I've always done that to her ever since she was teeny. "We're going to play at hairdressers, Maise!"

"Like in real life?" she asked.

"Yes, come and sit in this chair."

Archie screwed his face up at me. "Aren't you supposed to wash hair before you cut it?"

I thought he was probably right, but I was dying to get on with the actual cutting so I made something up. "Maisie's hair's quite flat. It'll be fine to cut it straight away."

Archie looked impressed and that made me feel quite clever, so as we were getting a towel to put round her shoulders I said something that I remembered the hairdresser once saying about my hair. "She's got quite a high crown...hmmm, I think I'll change the parting to make it hang better."

That made Archie look even more impressed.

We found some scissors in his chest of drawers. They'd got a bit of old dried-up glue on them, and I thought we ought to wash them, but Archie said they'd go rusty so I just had to hope they'd be all right. He let me wash his comb, though.

"You've got a lot of tangles, Maisie Griggs!" I said, as I started combing.

That made her giggle.

One of the knots was massive. I showed Archie. "This one's impossible to get out."

"That's where she twizzles it round her finger when she's sucking her thumb."

In the end I just cut the whole knot out because it would have taken the rest of the afternoon to untangle it, and it didn't show at all where the hair was missing. Well only a teeny bit anyway. Then I started snipping in a straight line across the bottom. It was tempting to take off a big chunk because it was such good fun, but Suky only wanted it trimmed, and I was determined to make sure I did it exactly how she wanted it. I was so looking forward to the look on her face when she saw what a helpful girl I'd been that I made myself stick to just one centimetre.

At least, I *think* it was a centimetre. I've never been all that good at measurements.

"Right, now for the fringe."

"I want to get down now," said Maisie.

"In a minute," I told her. "Nearly finished."

"But then there'll be none left for the hairdresser lady to do, silly Billie!"

"That's the whole idea, Maisie! We're going to save your mummy a lot of time and money, see."

It was quite tricky to see where the fringe started and where it finished because there were a few long strands hanging down and some medium ones, and some really wispy little bits. I'd just have to level it out to the shortest bit. That's probably what the hairdresser would have done.

"Can we play something else now?" said Maisie.

"Hurry up, Billie," said Archie. "Mum'll be coming up to get her soon."

And as he said that there was a ring at the front door.

"Who's that?" I asked.

"Dunno. Probably someone collecting money."

"Archie, can you bring Maisie down, please?"

came Suky's voice from downstairs. "The hairdresser's here to do her hair."

I froze. "Why didn't you tell me the hairdresser was coming *here*!"

"'Cos I didn't know, did I? She usually goes to the one in the High Street."

I closed my eyes and wished I could undo the whole haircut and go back to lunchtime. Now Suky was going to have to tell the hairdresser to go back home because there was no hair to cut after all. And the hairdresser would be cross because of wasting her time, and that would make Suky *very* cross. With me. Oh help!

"Did you hear me, Archie?" called Suky, a bit more loudly.

Then Maisie yelled out. "Billie's already—" but Archie clapped his hand over her mouth, and she didn't get any further.

"Ssh!" he said, whipping the towel off her shoulders and messing her hair up with his fingers. "Billie's only cut the teensiest bit off so there's no need to say anything to Mum or the hairdresser, all right? We don't want Mum to be cross, do we?"

"Is it a secret?" asked Maisie, her eyes all twinkly.

"Yes. Now get going," said Archie, shoving her through the door.

"Thanks, Arch," I whispered as we crept onto the landing, taking care to keep out of sight, and watched Maisie walking down clutching the banister.

"Come on, trouble," said Suky. "Say hello to Jenny."

"Hello, Maisie," said Jenny.

And my heart missed a beat because I recognized that voice. Jenny, the hairdresser... Of course. She lives just up the road from us. She's a friend of Mum's.

"Maisie!" Suky's voice was suddenly full of shock and crossness.

I'd never heard her sound like that before. I was leaning against the landing wall, but when I heard how mad she was I slid slowly down till I was sitting on the floor.

"Have you been cutting it yourself, Maisie? I told you never ever to use scissors."

I held my breath. Archie was pulling a *yikes!* face. It was all silent downstairs. If only I could see whether Maisie was giving the game away or not.

"Maisie! What's the matter? Answer me. Have you been cutting your hair?"

I bit my lip. I mean I really did bite it. I could taste the blood and everything.

Then Archie and I clearly heard Maisie's voice. "It's a secret."

I closed my eyes and felt sick.

"Archie, can you and Billie come down, please."

I might have got away with the Coke, but when I heard the coldness in Suky's voice I knew I was never going to get away with this. Why had everything gone wrong when I was trying so hard to be such a good daughterly sort of person?

"Dear me," came Jenny's voice. "Someone's had a good old hack round the back here. Maisie can't have done this herself, Suky. Not unless she's a contortionist!"

"Archie!"

This time Suky sounded really mad, and I just knew I couldn't bear it if she turned that crossness on me. Not now, when she was supposed to be adopting me. I'd have to try and get Archie to take the blame. It was my only hope.

"I can't go downstairs," I hissed at Archie. "The hairdresser knows my mum. What if she tells her what I did? Mum'd go mad. Can't you pretend that *you* cut Maisie's hair, Arch? Please, please, *please*!"

"But why should *I* get the blame when it was totally your idea?" Archie said in a hiss.

Then Suky called up to us again. Her voice was louder and a lot snappier this time. "Archie? Are you coming?"

"Oh go on, Arch," I begged. "Say I'm not feeling well." Then in the nick of time my brain came up with something perfect. "I'll give you all my pocket money."

I definitely saw his eyes light up a bit when I said that. "How much have you got?"

I didn't actually have *any*, because I'm not very good at saving up. I just spend my pocket money every week as soon as I get it. But that didn't matter. I'd work out how to get it later. The important thing was to make sure I said a big enough amount to make Archie think about that CD-ROM he wanted.

"Five pounds," I blurted out.

"On Monday, yeah?"

Impossible. I'd never do it... But I had no choice.

"Yeah."

"Shake on it then."

I shook.

In fact, to tell the truth, every bit of me shook.

7 The "Training" Part of the Plan

I went back into Archie's room, lay down on his bed and made myself think hard. Not my usual thought bubble, daydreamy stuff. Real hard thinking. I had to work things out more carefully from now on. I'd never wanted anything as big and important as to be adopted before, so it didn't matter if I made mistakes and got myself into a mess then. But from now on, I had to make sure I always thought carefully *before* I spoke, and also before I *did* things. Otherwise the parent plan would never work.

I was so deep in my thought bubble that I didn't even hear the bedroom door open, and it gave me a shock to see Suky standing there.

"Are you all right, Billie? Archie says you're not feeling well."

Her voice wasn't quite normal. But it couldn't have been because she wasn't happy with me. Archie would never have told her that it had really been me who had done Maisie's hair, not when we shook on the deal. I was certain of that. All the same, the sight of Suky's face without a smile on it made my heart beat faster.

"Erm…it's my stomach," I said quietly. Then I did a bit of a wince. "And also my head…"

She put her hand on my forehead and told me in a kind of brisk voice that I hadn't got a temperature. I thought about suggesting that she got the thermometer but decided that it might make her even brisker, and then what if the briskness turned into proper crossness? So I didn't say a single word, just lay there feeling miserable.

"I think I'd better phone your mum, Billie," said Suky frowning.

"No, it's okay…I mean I'll be all right if you don't mind me just lying here quietly."

"All right, then…" She turned to go but when

she was at the door she stopped and looked at me with narrowed eyes. "Billie…"

I waited with a stiff body.

"Maisie's hair…"

"Yes…" My voice seemed to have gone very thin.

"Archie says *he* did it."

"Yes…" I closed my eyes because it was easier than looking at her.

"And *did* he?"

My heart was getting louder as though it was talking to me strictly… *Don't tell her a lie. Don't tell her a lie.* But I had to. Just this once. Then never again after this one time.

"Yes, he did."

When I opened my eyes she'd gone. I lay there for a few seconds then got up and went over to the open window, still feeling miserable. But what I saw made my spirits rush up from the floor to the ceiling. Neil was walking round to the front of the house wearing a T-shirt, jogging bottoms and trainers. The only thing that was different from the dad in my daydream was that the T-shirt wasn't sweaty, but that was because he hadn't started running yet. It was obvious he was just about to though, because he was studying a stopwatch. Brilliant. Double brilliant. As soon as Neil got back I'd tell him all about my running and how I want to run in the Olympics when I grow up. He already knows I'm quite good because he usually comes to our sports days at school, but I wasn't sure if Archie had told him about the time when I did actually represent the school. I'd have to make sure he got to hear about that. And I'd tell him I'm planning on starting some serious training myself because I want to be in top fitness, and then I'd ask him if he'd like to time me.

I was well into a lovely thought bubble about Neil being proud of me for breaking my last running time by a whole five seconds when Archie's voice broke in.

"What are you looking at?" I hadn't even heard him come in.

"Your dad."

"How *very* interesting!"

Archie flopped down on the bed. I guessed he was sulking because of having to be told off for something he hadn't done. I suddenly felt really

really grateful to him and determined to give him the five pounds on Monday, even if it meant asking Mum for a double advance on my pocket money.

"Thanks for taking the blame, Arch. I'll definitely give you the five pounds on Monday."

He grunted and said it was okay, then sat down at his computer and gradually went back to his normal self, talking to me about a game we could play to see who got the highest score. I wasn't really listening properly because I was too wrapped up with thoughts about Neil and running.

"Does your dad always time himself when he runs, Arch?"

"Yeah… He's trying to get back into training. He used to run for the county, you know."

This was even better. He'd be such a great trainer and I absolutely couldn't wait to see what he said when he heard how keen I was on training to be as good as him. I could just imagine him smiling at me in a serious sort of way.

"You're quite a girl, aren't you, Billie?" he'd say.

And I'd keep perfectly quiet and look down. I wouldn't want him to think I was a show-off.

Everything was working out now and I hugged my precious idea to myself. It was definitely the best thing I'd thought of so far to do with my parent plan. As soon as I got home I'd write it all down and put it in my private box in my drawer.

Yesssss!

8 The Spear

On Sunday morning I woke up with a shock and sat bolt upright in bed. I'd just had a terrible dream about Maisie being completely bald because I'd combed her hair and it had all fallen out, and Suky had told me I was a horrible little girl and she didn't want to see me at her house ever again.

The dream felt so real that I couldn't shake it off until much later in the morning when Mum made me go and take a cup of tea to Quentin. He was in the back garden. When I looked through the kitchen window I saw him carving away at one of Mum's bamboo canes.

"Why doesn't he just stick the cane into the soil like it is? Why does he have to carve it?" I asked

Mum, already feeling irritated just at the sight of him.

"He's not gardening," said Mum with a bit of a mysterious look on her face that got on my nerves. "He's making a spear."

At first I thought I must still be asleep and in the middle of another weird dream. Why on earth would Quentin make a spear? He must be going a bit mad because of being so old.

"A spear! What for?"

"For fun."

No, Quentin never did anything for fun, unless it was one of Mum's ideas and he was just doing it to please her.

"Here you are, Billie," Mum said, handing me the tea. "Tell Quentin I've put the sugar in and stirred it."

As I went out of the back door I said to myself that I'd just give the cup of tea to Quentin then go straight back in the house.

"Thank you, Billie. Lovely! Just put it on that stone there."

"Mum's stirred it."

"Jolly good."

But it was weird because he didn't say anything about what he was doing. And that got me curious, so instead of going back in the house I sat down on the doorstep, not too close, and watched. There was something different about Quentin this morning. I couldn't work out what it was at first, then I realized it was the silence. For once, he wasn't humming. Good, because that humming of his really gets on my nerves, and I knew that the moment he started I'd have to go.

I watched him carving for a couple of minutes and noticed that the cane was beginning to get a really good point on the end of it. Then I wondered where he got the penknife from. I'd never seen it in our shed or in the house before.

After loads more silence he suddenly said, "We all carried penknives in our pockets when I was a boy, you know. Wouldn't be allowed now, I suppose, but I've kept mine. All these years."

I knew it was just a coincidence that Quentin had answered the very question I'd been thinking, but it did suddenly seem a bit spooky, all the same, like Quentin was a mind-reader or something. Or maybe

I'd actually managed to do that thought transference thing that Archie had told me about.

"This is going to fly like a javelin, Billie!"

"How do you know?"

"Because I've made plenty of these in my time, and they're the business!" He chuckled to himself, then gave me one of his *Aren't we having fun?* smiles, but I didn't smile back because I was thinking how silly he looked with a penknife at his age. Neil wouldn't have looked silly. But Neil wouldn't have had one in the first place. It was too old-fashioned.

I wanted to ask Quentin why he'd suddenly decided to make a spear *now*, but I thought one question was enough, or he might think I was more interested than I really was. Then the dreaded humming started and after about ten seconds it made my muscles go into knots so I decided to go inside and come back out later when the spear might be finished.

"Now, Billie, can you ask your mum for a piece of cardboard?" He smiled at the sky. "We used to use cereal packets when I was a boy, you know."

I wished he'd stop saying *when I was a boy*. It only kept reminding me how old he was.

"And don't forget a pair of scissors, Billie!"

Oh great! So now I'd got to come back out straight away.

Then he gave me one of his winks. But it looked stupid because Quentin just isn't a winking sort of person. If Neil had winked it would have looked really cool. In the kitchen I found the Weetabix packet and took the inside of it out, then went back into the garden with the cardboard bit and the scissors. I'd made a plan to tell Quentin I was going to the loo, then I'd stay inside for about half an hour. That'd give him time to finish the spear, and I wouldn't have to hang around listening to him going on and on about when he was a boy.

"Right, this is the flight, Billie. You've got to be careful with this part." He was cutting out a square of cardboard and folding it in all different directions.

Maybe I'd just watch for a little while then. At least he'd stopped humming. Next he carved a cross in one end of the cane so it fanned out in four quarters, then he started stuffing the folded cardboard into the cross. I couldn't work out how he'd got it to stay wedged in there so I went to have a closer look.

"Oh I get it. It's a bit like a dart."

He nodded. "That's right... Now, you see how carefully I'm making these little notches...ferrules, we used to call them... Pop and get some string, and some cotton to secure the flight, eh, Billie?"

Quentin sounded so stupid when he talked, as though he didn't know how to talk to a ten-year-old girl. But he ought to really, because Victoria was ten once, wasn't she? Neil was used to girls because of Maisie and used to ten-year-olds because of Archie. So that would be fine when I was adopted. Actually he was used to eleven-year-olds too because Archie was nearly a whole year older than me. In fact he was one of the oldest in Year Six, and I was just about the youngest, so people wouldn't think it odd when they heard we were brother and sister.

Mum was in the sitting room having a clear-up when I went in to get the cotton from her sewing drawer.

"Is it good, Billie?"

She was smiling away, and I wasn't sure if she

meant is it good watching Quentin, or is the spear good, so I just shrugged and said, "'T's all right," then went back outside.

"Okay, this is going to travel a fair old distance, Billie, so let's go!"

And before I knew it he'd opened the back door and called out to Mum that we were going to Pudding Hill, then started striding off round the front.

"Can't we just do it here…?"

"Nope. We need a nice open space. Come on. We'll take the car. There's not much time before lunch."

I'd never been anywhere in the car with just Quentin before, and I didn't really want to now, partly in case anyone saw me with him, but mainly because I didn't want to have to talk to him.

Pudding Hill turned out to be exactly four minutes and nineteen seconds away in the car. I know that because I watched the clock in the car the whole way. Quentin had a CD on and it was the same music I kept hearing at home.

"This is the foxtrot, Billie. My favourite."

He hummed with the music, and it came out

much louder than his normal humming, but at least it was better than having to talk.

We pulled in at a gravelly car-park bit at the bottom of the hill and got out of the car. I opened the gate and Quentin told me it was called a kissing gate. Neil would never have bothered to mention something as boring as that. And anyway if I'd been with Neil we would have both been too puffed out for any talking because we'd have run all the way here.

When we'd gone through the gate and walked along a bit we had our backs to the road and were looking up the hill. The reason it's called Pudding Hill is that it's like a Christmas pudding, round, with a flat top.

Quentin seemed really excited about his spear. I watched him put the knotted end of the string in a little notch that he'd cut, up near the flight. "See that, Billie?" Then he lined it up along the side of the cane. "Right, you have to wrap the rest round your hand." He helped me. "That's right. Now get ready to hurl it as hard as you can. Get set... Go!"

I did as he said and the spear shot out into the air and glided along for ages. I couldn't believe

I'd managed to send it so far. We both shielded our eyes and watched it land up near the top of the hill. It was wicked.

"Hey, cool!" I wasn't thinking about Quentin any more. Only about the spear. "I'll go and get it."

"Nice throw, Billie. Good technique."

I started to run up the hill and suddenly understood why dogs like chasing sticks. My legs ached by the time I got to the top because I'd run so fast. I looked down and saw that Quentin was beckoning to me to come down to the bottom again.

When I got back down to him he said that it was best to only send it from the bottom of the hill to the top and not in the other direction or it might go on the road. I thought he was probably right about that because it could fly a really long distance.

"Right, my turn now," he said, lining the string up and wrapping it round his hand. "And now for the moment of truth…"

Wham! The spear shot off so fast that I couldn't see it at first. Then I saw it – miles away. It went on and on, up and up, until it was right out of sight.

"Wow! It *has* gone over the other side!"

"Yep, I reckon it has, unless it's somewhere on the flat top."

"I'll go and see."

"Thank goodness for your speedy running, Billie. My old legs wouldn't make it up that hill very well!"

I wished he hadn't said that. I'd forgotten about him being old for a few minutes there, and now he'd spoiled things again.

"Fly it from wherever it's landed, Billie," he called out. "There won't be any danger of it going on the road from right over there."

My legs felt heavier climbing the hill this second time, and when I got to the top there was no sign of the spear so I ran across till I could see the other side, and there it was, about halfway down. It had gone for miles! I couldn't wait to fly it back to Quentin, to see if I could make it go as far as he had done, and I was just about to rush down and get it when I stopped in my tracks. Every drop of excitement dissolved into nothingness because I'd caught sight of who was at the hedge at the bottom. Surrounded by his friends, drinking from a can. Liam Compton.

He saw me straight away and yelled up the hill. "Oi! Billie! What yer doing?"

I had to get the spear and get it fast. So I raced down the hill, nearly falling over I was going so quickly. Liam didn't move at first and I was whispering under my breath, saying, "*Stay there, Liam, stay there.*" Then when I got to the spear and picked it up he called out. "What yer got, Billie? Let's have a look." And a second later he was rushing up towards me with Tom and Isaac, Josh and Ben all following.

It was so tempting to just run away as fast as my legs would carry me, but that would only make Liam curious, and he might follow me back down to Quentin. No way could I let that happen, so I picked up the spear with fumbling fingers and stood there trying with all my might to act casual so Liam would think it wasn't anything worth looking at, and he'd leave me alone.

"What's it supposed to be?" he asked, taking it from me and frowning as he turned it over and over.

"It's quite clever, isn't it?" said Josh. "Who made it then?"

"Not *Billie*, that's pretty obvious," sniggered Liam.

The others joined in the laughter and my heart sank. This wasn't how the conversation was supposed to be going.

"It's nothing much, actually. I got it from… Archie…"

"Is Archie over there, then?" asked Tom. "Shall we fly it back to him?"

"No… I came on my own. Anyway, I've got to go now." I took the spear off him, trying like mad to keep up my casual act, and set off walking, my heart beating hard and a little prayer going on inside my head. *Please don't let him follow me. Please don't let him follow me.*

He didn't. But something much worse happened. Quentin suddenly appeared on the top of the hill, and the blood drained from my face.

"Thought I'd give you a hand," he called.

"Wooo, Billie told a lie!" came Liam's horrible sneery voice, just loud enough for me to hear. "You're not on your own, are you? You're with your granddad. Doesn't sound very Australian to me."

The other boys laughed out loud as I ran off. I saw a look of confusion come over Quentin's face. He must have heard that last bit, and it made me feel suddenly mean and horrible. But then I remembered that I wouldn't have to be here worrying about Liam stupid Compton if Quentin hadn't met Mum in the first place. So I don't know why I was feeling sorry. It was all his fault.

"I'm hungry. Let's go," I said, rushing past him.

"Oh..." He sounded shocked and sad, but I didn't care. At least he was following me back down to the road.

"Friends of yours?" he asked when we were near the bottom.

I didn't look at him. "They're in my class." Then I just had to take a quick glance so I could be quite sure they hadn't followed me down. But they had, and my stomach turned over at the way they were swaggering down the hill with big smirks all over their faces.

All I wanted to do was to get away now. *Right* now. And Quentin must have kind of understood because he was striding off towards the car.

"We can come back another time, Billie," he said.

It was a big relief in one way, but in another way I felt stupid because it was obvious I was scared of Liam and the others. And feeling stupid makes me cross.

I stared at the ground as I followed Quentin to the car, and we were only a few metres from it when we heard a tooting and saw the blue Fiesta that Mum and Victoria share.

"Looks like we've got company, Billie," said Quentin, smiling at the car turning into the car park.

My heart sank as Victoria pulled up next to Quentin's car, because Liam and the others were coming through the kissing gate now.

"Hello, darling!" said Quentin.

Victoria got out of her car. "Hello, Daddy. I've been sent to tell you it's time for lunch." She looked at the spear in my hand and then at me. "Had fun, Billie? Done a bit of father-daughter bonding? He's a jolly good dad when it comes to spears, isn't he!" She laughed and I wanted to shrink to the size of a marble and roll away down the drain because I knew that Liam and the others were right behind me now.

Quentin chuckled as he unlocked the car and got in. "We're on our way!"

Liam was strolling past me. He turned round and raised his eyebrows. "So he's not your granddad then, Billie." His voice was low and mean. "He's your *real* dad or your stepdad or something. You were telling lies, weren't you?"

I felt like screaming and crying all at once. It wasn't fair. Nothing was fair. My blood was boiling and the words were out of my mouth before I could stop them. "He's not *any* kind of dad, for your information!"

And that's when Quentin's door slammed shut, and I realized he must have heard what I'd said.

It was like I was in a tunnel and the words kept bouncing off the walls and coming right back at me, again and again, only the echoes got louder instead of quieter. Victoria pursed her lips tight, then got back in her car without a word and drove off. Liam carried on strolling down the road, and I stared straight ahead with my head bursting until I couldn't bear it any longer. Then I chucked the stupid spear on the ground and ran off in the opposite direction from Liam, towards home.

When I looked back after a minute I saw that Quentin hadn't even switched his engine on. He was just sitting there. I didn't care.

I didn't care about anything except getting away from him.

For ever.

9 The Terrible Thought

I went in through the back door, wishing more than ever that I could get on with my parent plan so I didn't have to live here or have anything to do with *this* family for another single minute. Mum wasn't in the kitchen, thank goodness, and neither was Victoria. But her car was here, and lunch was on the table. Salad and quiche and ham and new potatoes. I wasn't at all hungry. It was like all the feelings and thoughts in my head were making me full already, so there wasn't room for anything else.

I went straight upstairs, shut my bedroom door and sat on the floor, leaning against the wall with my knees up, but no matter how tightly I pulled them in to me it didn't feel tight enough. I buried my head and wished I could bury all the thoughts too, but they wouldn't be buried because they were pounce thoughts, only they weren't exactly pouncing, they were standing up on their hind legs and snarling.

It wasn't *my* fault. We shouldn't have gone to Pudding Hill in the first place. But it wouldn't have made any difference if we'd gone somewhere else. You never know where Liam Compton's going to pop up. I wish he'd move away and take his stupid gang with him. Then I could go to secondary in September and I wouldn't have to worry about having a pathetic old granddad for a stepdad. Except that I *would*, wouldn't I, because they have parents' evenings and sports days and things at secondary as well as primary, don't they? And Quentin would go with Mum, and everyone would stare, and then they'd start on me.

I lifted my foot and banged it down hard on the floor. I hoped Mum was back in the kitchen, and I'd given her a shock. It was all her fault. She didn't think about me for one second when she married Quentin, did she? I heard a car draw up outside. So he was back, was he? Well, he needn't think I was going to talk to him. Or Victoria. Or Mum. They couldn't make me. And anyway, I'd be out of here soon. Adopted into a proper nice *young* family. I couldn't wait for the next step in my plan.

"Wash your hands, Billie. It's lunchtime."

I raised my head and yelled out, "I'm not hungry."

But I was by then. Even with all the thoughts still crashing about inside my head, I could feel my stomach starving.

Then I heard footsteps on the stairs, and I knew it was Victoria. I bet she was coming to talk to me. Well, tough toffees!

"Billie, can I come in?"

"No."

But she just ignored me and came in anyway, then she bobbed down in front of me and tried to make me look at her. I looked the other way, so then she put her hand on my knee. And that's when I stood up and went over to my window.

"Billie…" She was talking to my back. "…we all understand that you're finding it difficult having a new stepdad…"

"No, you don't actually."

"Well, *help* us to understand then. Tell us what's the matter... Then we can try and help. Poor Daddy's just got back and he looks so upset."

For some reason my crossness seemed to have turned into a big sadness, and I thought I might cry if I said anything so I stayed silent and kept blinking and swallowing to stop tears from coming.

"Daddy said you loved the spear, and it was only when those boys from your class appeared that you got embarrassed. But there's nothing to be embarrassed about. They're horrible, and you just have to ignore them."

She put her hand on my shoulder, but I shook it off because it was only making the lump in my throat hurt more. And that got me back into my angry mood again, so I stomped out of the room yelling out, "You don't know anything about *anything*!"

Then I ran downstairs and nearly knocked Mum over when I got to the bottom.

"Hold it right there!" She grabbed my shoulders and steered me really quickly backwards into the kitchen. Then she pushed my shoulders down, and I found myself in a chair. I don't think I've ever seen her looking so mad. "You will sit there, and you will eat."

I felt really stupid because Quentin was sitting at the table too, helping himself to quiche as though everything was completely normal. And then Victoria came in and sat down as well, and Mum smiled at her and they started talking about something they'd seen on telly the night before. And Mum said what a nice top Victoria was wearing and asked her if she had any plans for the afternoon. And then Quentin put some quiche and new potatoes and salad on my plate, and next thing Victoria was passing me the bread rolls but I shook my head even though I knew Mum would be looking at me. She couldn't force me to eat a bread roll, could she?

That meal was the worst meal of my life. I only ate it to stop Mum having another go at me. The three grown-ups talked as though I wasn't even there, and I felt like the biggest odd-man-out or odd-*person*-out ever. It was three against one round that table, and I knew for certain that it would always be three against one if I stayed in this family. But I wasn't staying, was I? Thinking about the parent plan made a little puff of happiness nestle into the solid block of anger inside my head.

The spear was sitting on the dresser, I noticed, with the flight all bent up. That must have happened when I chucked it on the ground.

"So it worked all right," Mum said, out of the blue, as though she could read my mind.

I felt my heart speeding up.

"Oh yes, it worked a treat," said Quentin, smiling at her. "Went for miles."

Victoria suddenly laughed. "Do you remember all those spears you made for me, Daddy?"

Quentin gave a little chuckle. "And no matter how big they were, you simply weren't interested, were you?"

Victoria was still giggling. "Even when you stuck those pink feathers on the end…"

"Do you know, I'd forgotten about that one!"

Then Quentin suddenly stopped laughing and stared at the wall. I followed his eyes to see what he was looking at, but there was nothing there. I thought he must be in a daydream, and I wondered what he was thinking about. It was weird to think that he'd made spears for Victoria when she was a little girl and she'd not liked them at all. And now he'd made another one, and *I* didn't like it. Well, I *did*. I mean there was nothing wrong with the actual spear...

And before I knew it I'd slid into a thought bubble wondering if Quentin had been secretly looking forward to having a stepdaughter who wasn't all girlie like Victoria – someone a bit tomboyish like me who could appreciate his spears. But I got rid of that bubble quickly. So what if he *did*? I didn't want *him* as a stepfather.

I must have looked as though I was going to say something, though, because Mum and Victoria were both leaning forwards, looking at me, waiting.

"What, Billie?" said Victoria in her gentle voice.

"Nothing." I glared at her.

After lunch Mum made me clear the whole table and load up the dishwasher. It was obvious she was still mad with me, but she didn't talk about what had happened, thank goodness. Then I went up to my room and stared out of the window and saw the daisies on the lawn and thought of Neil making daisy chains for Maisie. That was such a lovely thing to do.

Maybe I'd give Archie a quick ring and see if I could go round to his house after school one day next week, as there was absolutely no chance I'd be able to go today. I'd make sure it was a day when Suky and Neil were both definitely going to be there, though.

"Hey, Arch, it's me."

"Hey. What yer doing?"

"Nothing much." Then I lowered my voice, just in case. "Guess who I've just seen at Pudding Hill."

"Give up."

"Liam and Tom and the others."

"What were you doing at Pudding Hill?"

"Flying a spear with Quentin. He made it."

"Hey, cool! You're so lucky, Billie. I've been to a boring old garden centre with Mum and Dad."

"Yeah, but Archie, don't you get it? Liam was there. He saw me with Quentin, and he knows he's not my granddad now. It was awful. I ran all the way home."

"That's good. It means you don't have to worry any more about Liam finding out from the newspaper, do you?"

I'd never thought of it like that…

"So what was the spear like?"

"Just…like a normal spear really. But it went quite far."

I didn't want to talk about the spear because it was part of such a horrible memory, and anyway I was still staring out of the window at the daisies on the lawn and that gave me another great brainwave. This one was inspirational.

"What kind of flowers does your mum like, Arch?"

"Flowers? Dunno."

"Only I was thinking of buying her some as a present – to make up for cutting Maisie's hair and giving her the Coke."

"She just likes normal flowers, you know, from a shop. But flowers cost loads, Billie. You don't have to bother."

My heart sunk. There was no way I could afford to spend loads on flowers. I couldn't even afford to pay Archie the five pounds I owed him. There was a bit of a silence while I thought about that again. Things were so bad between Mum and me that there was definitely absolutely no way she was going to advance me any pocket money now. But Archie must have been doing his thought transference thing again because he suddenly said, "You know the five pounds that you owe me…"

"Yeah."

"Well, it's okay. You don't have to pay me. Mum says those CD-ROMs about the endangered species are educational, and now Grandma wants to buy me the other one, so I don't need the money after all."

Those words made a sudden surge of big gratefulness well up in me. Archie was just the best best friend anyone could have. He could have easily taken my money and not said anything about his grandma getting him the CD-ROM. A second later the big gratefulness turned to massive happiness at the memory that he'd soon be even better than a best friend. He'd be my brother. It was going to be so cool.

When I put the phone down I was still excited. I'd forgotten all about arranging to go round to Archie's during the week, but that didn't matter. I could do it the next day at school. For now I wanted to think about flowers for Suky. The daisies on the lawn looked so teeny-weeny. But I was going to buy big flowers. Big red tulips standing up tall and thin like models. Perfect for the perfect parent in my perfect parent plan. And Suky would think I was such a nice, sweet, thoughtful girl. I could just imagine the look on her face when she saw them. She'd probably give me a kiss. I didn't think Suky had ever kissed me before. She might have done when I was little, I suppose. All she gives me these days is hugs. Kisses are more motherly things. Motherly-daughterly things. I like those words.

But I'd only got as far as the bedroom door when I realized the big problem. I didn't have any money, did I? Just because Archie was letting me off the five pounds, it didn't mean that I was five pounds richer. I'd still got absolutely nothing. I was right back to mad again. Stupid old Mum! Stupid old Victoria! Stupid old ancient antique dinosaur Quentin! I started ransacking my room in a big temper. I opened all my drawers to check if there might be any coins left in them by mistake – even a little five-pence piece. But there wasn't a single penny. And I probably needed at least five pounds.

Archie said shop flowers cost loads. I just *had* to get the flowers, though, now I'd had the idea. But then a terrible thought came into my head and even though I tried to shake it away, it wouldn't go.

You could steal the money, Billie.

Stealing's not right. It's...like a proper crime.

But no one would find out.

They might.

You only need to take a bit from each person, not a lot from the same person.

But stealing's not right.

I was back where I started. So I went through the whole thing again inside my head, only this time I stopped when I got to the part about only taking a bit from each person.

Suppose I did... Just suppose... How would I do it?

I could take about one pound fifty or two pounds from all the three grown-ups. Mum would be the easiest because she doesn't know what she's got in her purse half the time. Victoria would be the next easiest because she's always leaving her money lying around, and I reckon if I just took a bit here and a bit there she'd never notice. Quentin would be the hardest to steal from because even though I know he's got the most money, I've never actually seen any of it. I only ever hear it jangling in his trouser pocket… Hmmm. That got me thinking… First thing in the morning when he's shaving and Mum's downstairs making breakfast, his trousers must be in the bedroom.

And that was the moment I decided to carry out my terrible plan. I'd do it the very next morning. It would be scary, but worth it.

Definitely worth it. To get adopted. That's what I kept telling myself.

10 The Letter

I didn't quite have enough courage to carry out the stealing plan the next morning after all. I think it was because I needed so much courage for school. I was dreading going into the classroom and seeing Liam, so I hung about on the edge of the playground for ages after Mum had dropped me off.

In the end the bell went and I *had* to go in. I straight away looked round for Archie, but he must have gone for the register because that's his job.

"Hey, Billie, how's your old man?"

Liam had spoken in such a loud voice that everyone had stopped what they were doing to listen in.

Please hurry up and come back, Archie.

"D'you get it?" Liam carried on, grinning round the classroom. "*Old* man!"

All the people in his gang started laughing. And they laughed even more when Liam suddenly started walking round the classroom wiggling his hips and wearing a stupid pouty expression on his face. "This is Billie's big sister, right…" He put on a high-pitched posh voice, "Oooh Daddy, what a soooooper little spear!"

The gang were laughing their heads off by then, and even the girls in the class were smiling at each other. I suddenly felt a big temper coming up in me.

"It's better than anything *you* could make actually!"

I couldn't believe that those words had come out of my mouth. I hadn't told my brain to make my mouth say that. But I'd said it, and I felt pleased with myself for a moment because Liam looked pretty surprised and so did a few other people too. And just after that Archie and the teacher came back in.

"Sit in your places, please," said Mrs. Palmer. "I'm about to take the register so could I have silence."

It must be so cool being a teacher. You could just

clap your hands and ask for silence. If only I could do that every time Liam Compton opened his horrible big mouth.

Silence, Liam Compton.

It would be wicked.

The more Liam went on about Quentin and Victoria, the more I wanted to punish them for spoiling my life. *And* Mum. Why shouldn't I take money from all three of them? It would make things a bit fairer after what they'd made me put up with, wouldn't it?

The trouble was I never got the chance. You see, Victoria must have suddenly turned very tidy because she seemed to have stopped leaving her money lying around. Then there was Mum. Her purse was in her handbag and her handbag was in the kitchen, but it was like she'd alarmed it, because every time I went anywhere near it, she appeared.

So that left Quentin. Well, I'd sneaked into his and Mum's room when he'd been shaving, and seen his money on the chest of drawers. At first I'd thought I was in luck, but then I'd seen that there weren't any pound coins or fifty-pence pieces, there were only two twenty-pound notes and a few two-pence and one-pence pieces.

At that moment I nearly decided to forget all about getting flowers for Suky because it was turning out to be such a complicated thing to do. But I couldn't help picturing her smiling at the tulips, saying, "Mmm, lovely! These are my favourites, you know, Billie!" Then she'd ask me to help her arrange them (after she'd kissed me, that is). But that bit of the thought bubble wasn't quite right because you don't need two people to arrange tulips, do you? You could just stick them in a vase. So maybe a big higgledy-piggledy bunch of flowers with leaves and everything would be better. Yes, and we'd both be laughing together because we'd keep on dropping bits on the floor. Then it would be like the time when Victoria dropped a postcard behind the bookshelves, and she and Mum tried to move the shelves but all the books kept falling out, and they were laughing so much they had to give up till they'd calmed down.

After the flower bubble, my mind went sliding along a whole string of thoughts until it had formed another totally cool plan. And this was it. I could run from my house all the way to Archie's with the flowers. I'd explain to Neil and Suky that I'd run my very fastest because of not wanting the flowers to be out of water for too long so they wouldn't die. And that's when I'd tell Neil I was starting some serious training and he'd be really interested and very impressed. Yes! Great plan, Billie!

But then the pounce thought came crashing in. It wasn't a great plan. It was a stupid plan with a big fat fault in it. I couldn't do that running thing, could I, because Mum would never let me. It's so unfair. Just because Archie's house hasn't got any other houses nearby, Mum says it's too remote and out in the country, and she goes on about the road being dangerous and winding, and how it's even worse because of there not being any pavement for some of the way.

But, wait a minute… What if I told Mum I was going out training somewhere near our house? She'd never know I'd been over to Archie's as long as I only stayed a little while. And if anyone saw me while I was out I could pretend that Mum had changed her mind now I was nearly eleven, and she didn't mind me going to Archie's on my own.

Then it would be time for the very best part of the whole plan. Even thinking about it made me come out in goose bumps. Just before I went back home, I was going to give Suky a letter from me and ask her to read it in private after I'd gone. It would explain all about how well I'd fit into her family, and what a nice daughter I'd be if she and Neil adopted me. And I'd thought of loads of good ways to say that in the letter. Right. Brilliant. Sorted. I'd start with the stealing and get that bit over with first.

When I went into the kitchen Mum was just going outside with a black bin liner full of rubbish to put in the wheelie bin. Her handbag was in its usual place on the back of the chair. Victoria was out, and Quentin was doing some kind of work in the living room. There was a whole pile of letters on the desk so it looked as though he might be there for a while. If I was going to steal this money I had to do it right now.

Okay, Billie, it's now or never!

I looked right and left, feeling a bit like a robber in a film, then I got Mum's purse out. It was quite heavy.

Good. In the zipped bit there were two fifty-pence coins, two pound coins, and some other change. I didn't even bother to check if she'd got any notes, just took out one of the pound coins and a fifty-pence piece. She'd never notice in a million years because the purse didn't look any different with those two coins missing. I quickly zipped it up and put it back exactly where I'd found it, then rushed up to my bedroom with my heart beating loud and fast.

This was easy-peasy. It must be a good omen. I crept back out onto the landing and listened at the top of the stairs to check where Mum was. I couldn't hear her anywhere so I went into Victoria's room. I must say it was very messy indeed. If *my* room had been in this much of a mess Mum would have been totally stressed out and made me tidy it up, so how come Victoria was allowed to get away with it?

I looked on the dressing table, the chest of drawers and the windowsill, but there wasn't any money. I looked all over the floor, the bed and the bedside table. Still nothing. So then I started on her clothes. She'd left two pairs of jeans, a denim jacket and another jacket lying around. Those were the only things with pockets. I checked them all. Only I was starting to get scared that Mum might suddenly come in and I couldn't think of a single reason why I might be in Victoria's room so I nearly ran out. But then I suddenly spotted a pair of jogging bottoms that I knew she wore for aerobics in her washing basket. I pulled them out, stuck my hand in the zip pocket and felt something cold. It was a pound coin. Brilliant! And even better than brilliant, she'd obviously forgotten she'd left it in there. Perfect!

So now I'd got two pounds fifty. Yahoo! The next day I'd try Quentin again, but for now all I had to do was whizz back to my room and write the letter. I'd been expecting it to take quite a while and be full of crossings out, but I gave myself a surprise because I did it in about five minutes, and the writing was really neat.

Dear Suky and Neil,

I know your going to be shocked when you get this but I hope it will be a good kind of shock. My mum probably thought it would be fine to marry Quentin but she didn't realize hes two old for a girl like me (not like you, Neil!). In fact hes like a granddad and evryone at school teases me about it. Mum and Quentin and Victoria are all grown ups together and they woud'nt miss me if I lived in another family like yours. Ive always wanted a brother and a sister and a dog, by the way, and I would try to be a perfect daughter. (I'm quite a fast runner, Neil, and I thought you might like to time me running, and I could time you if you want). I'd be the hapiest girl in the world if you said I could join in your family. Thank you very much indeed.

Love and best wishes from your (hopefuly) adopted daughter!

Billie GRIGGS!!!

When I'd read through the letter twice I put it in an old envelope that had once had a birthday card in it. It said *BILLIE* on the front so I just wrote to *TO SUKY FROM* in front of the word Billie and stuck a bit of Sellotape over the flap of the envelope. It was rather manky Sellotape because it was the very end of the roll, but it would have to do. I was sure Suky wouldn't mind about the outside of the envelope. It was what was written on the inside that was important, after all.

My whole body shivered with excitement when I thought about her reading it. I could just imagine her calling out to Neil and both of them looking at it together. They might have tears in their eyes, but they'd be tears of happiness. And they'd probably turn to each other and say: "*What an amazing girl Billie is to have worked out such an incredible plan. It really does make perfect sense. Of course we'll adopt her.*"

11 The Race Against Time

When I woke up on Thursday morning I felt brilliant straight away. I think it was another sign that everything was about to be sorted in my life.

I jumped out of bed and got dressed, then the moment I heard Quentin go in the bathroom I sneaked into his and Mum's bedroom. I looked on the chest of drawers and got the biggest *kapow!* feeling in the world. There were loads of coins and a couple of notes. Faster than the fastest burglar I took two pounds fifty and spread out the rest of the coins a bit to make it look like there were more, then I sneaked out and dived back into my room. I put Quentin's money with Mum's and Victoria's in a little box that used to have an ornament in it, and hid the box at the very back of my cupboard that's got all my stuff in it. Mum would never find it there, and the other two never even went into my room.

When I was standing behind Archie in the queue for assembly, I suddenly felt a big urge to tell him my whole plan, otherwise he'd be the last to know, and that didn't seem all that fair when he was my best friend and could-be-brother. But still the little voice inside me was saying: *What if Archie doesn't think it's a good idea?* So I decided to keep quite for a little while longer. After all it would only be a *very* little while now. And that reminded me...

"Archie, can I bring the flowers over to your mum later?"

But even as I was saying that I was realizing something. How was I actually going to buy the flowers? Mum would never let me go into town on my own. It was too far, and I couldn't ask her to buy the flowers *for* me. I couldn't even ask Victoria because she'd want to know who they were for. I was cross with myself for not working out this important part of the plan properly. And of course that got me mad with Mum and Quentin again.

The day didn't get any better either. Mrs. Palmer had a go at me in Literacy, because she didn't like my poem, which was totally unfair of her. I'd done really neat writing and used loads of imagination, and all she could say was that I'd rushed it too much and hadn't searched hard enough inside my brain for the best possible words to use.

"Think of it like this, Billie. Every time you write something down, it automatically becomes more important than just saying it."

I knew that already. I'd proved it with my adoption letter. Suky was going to be so surprised, but pleased too, because it's not every day that someone chooses your family to get adopted into. She'd probably want a massive celebration with champagne and everything.

At half past six I put on my tracksuit and stuffed the letter in one pocket and the money in another. I'd done a lot of thinking and had decided to let Archie get his mum the flowers at the weekend when his family went shopping together. I'd made him double promise to get red tulips and to explain to Suky that they were from me. I could have given him the five pounds at school the next day but it might have got stolen (which I know is a bit of a funny thing to say, considering I'd stolen it in the first place) so it was safer to give it to him now. And actually this giving-the-money-to-Archie plan was probably *better* than the flower plan because I'd be able to run faster if I wasn't carrying a bunch of flowers, and that meant Neil would be even more impressed. So this was definitely going to be the most important part of the parent plan. I could hardly stop my excitement from showing. I felt as though little giggles were sprouting out all over me, and I had to hug myself to keep them inside.

Mum was doing something at the sink.

I tried to make my voice as normal as possible. "I'm going jogging, Mum. Is that okay?"

"Jogging? Where?"

"Just round here. But I might jog round and round for quite a while. I want to get in training, you see."

"What for?"

"'Cos it's good for you."

She gave me a big smile. "You're right there. Maybe I ought to come with you!"

"No, you wouldn't be able to keep up, Mum."

"Don't look so worried, love, I was only joking."

Phew!

Then she looked at her watch and frowned. "I want you back here at seven thirty at the very latest, all right, Billie?"

I nodded. "Can I quickly phone Archie first, though, to remind him about a book he's supposed to be bringing into school tomorrow?"

Mum wasn't concentrating on me any more. She was pulling bits out of the plughole in the sink with a disgusted look on her face.

"Yes, okay."

So I went in the living room and tapped in Archie's number. I didn't really have to remind him about a book, I just wanted to make sure that Neil was going to be there so he'd see how fast I could run.

And then I got an extra brainwave. "Can you ask your dad how long he reckons it'd take me to run all the way from my house to yours?"

"I thought you weren't allowed."

I so nearly told him the truth again, but if he thought I was doing something a bit dangerous he might tell his mum or dad. That's what Archie's like.

"Mum says it's okay, now I'm practically eleven."

"Yeah, it's your birthday on Monday, isn't it?"

I'd forgotten all about my birthday. Usually, I think about it every second of every minute of every day of every week from when it's about two months away. This year was different though. I had something more important to think about this year.

Archie was talking to his dad, but I could hear what he was saying. "How long d'you reckon it'd take to run from Billie's house to here, Dad?"

"I dunno… Depends how fast you were running. About fifteen minutes, maybe?"

The moment I put the phone down I called bye to Mum and set off.

Just watch this then, Neil… You're going to see a champion runner coming up your drive in fourteen minutes!

Unfortunately I think I set off a bit too fast, and I nearly bashed into an old lady as I was flying round a corner. You see, Archie's house suddenly seemed an awfully long way away if I'd only got fourteen minutes. I wasn't sure that Neil had really thought carefully enough about how long it ought to take, but I was determined to do it even though a stitch was already forming in my side.

I decided to go into a thought bubble to help make the journey go faster, so I did the one about Neil timing me, waiting at his gate with the stopwatch and calling out to me in a really excited voice to run harder so I'd break my last record. That was a great thought bubble, but it got broken off because a car came round the bend at top speed, and I had to press myself into the hedge.

There were loads of bends on this road and hardly any pavement. No wonder Mum thought it was dangerous. During the worst bendy bit I had to stay right next to the hedge the whole time.

When I'd been running for eight minutes it still seemed like quite a way to go, and my stitch was getting worse. Also I felt boiling hot because the sun hadn't started setting yet. So then I started imagining Sports Day at school in Year Seven, and me coming first, and Neil, Suky, Archie and Maisie all cheering their heads off. That was a lovely thought bubble to be in. I did think about Mum too, but I couldn't work out whether she should be with Quentin or not so I left her out altogether, and then I felt horrible so I put her back in with Quentin and had them watching me from a bit further away. It wouldn't matter at all about Liam seeing them because he'd know that they weren't anything to do with me any more.

Archie's got two gates – one for cars and one for people. I was on twelve minutes thirty seconds when I first saw them, and I would have patted myself on the back but I didn't want to waste any energy. My whole body felt trembly with running so hard and my stitch was agony. It was thirteen minutes fifteen seconds when I went hurtling through the people gate at top speed and made it bash against the wall by mistake. That didn't matter now, though. Neil was going to be so impressed. I couldn't help a little giggle of happiness coming out amongst all my puffing at that moment. Then I used up my very last bit of energy running up the drive, which is quite steep.

Gorky came a little way down to meet me, barking his head off, and that seemed like another good omen. Even Gorky could sense that something brilliant was about to happen. (I have heard that dogs really can sense things like that.) I didn't bend down to give him a pat, though, because I didn't want to waste a single second. I just raced on up the drive and across the pebbly bit at the top, where they park their cars, to the front door. Suky's car wasn't there, but she'd probably be back soon. I looked at my watch as I rang the bell. Fourteen minutes thirty-two seconds. Yessss!

Come on. Hurry up…

"Hi!" Archie was opening the door wide for me to go in. "You're sweating like mad, Billie! And you're redder than Rudolph the Reindeer's nose. In fact you're even redder than—"

"Can you just tell your dad I'm here?"

"Eh?" He was looking puzzled.

"Just tell him, okay!"

I pushed past him and nearly fell onto the hall floor. Archie shut the front door and called out, but Neil didn't appear.

"I think he's on the phone."

I was so fed up, all I could do was thrust my watch under Archie's nose and wheeze, "Fourteen thirty-two…"

He seemed to stare at the watch for ages with his nose wrinkled right up. "No, it's not, it's 19:04," he said in the end. "And what are we suddenly talking in twenty-four-hour clock for anyway?"

I didn't know what he was on about. "Just tell your dad it took me fourteen minutes thirty-two, okay?"

Anyone'd think I'd asked him to tell his dad I'd come on the back of a pig the way he was looking at me. I thought he might act a bit more normally if I gave him the five pounds so I handed it over and reminded him it was for flowers for his mum.

"Oh yeah." He stuffed it in his pocket as though it was four pence or something and said he was right in the middle of a really good computer game in his room.

"Come and see it if you want."

I thought I'd just stay for a minute or two, then Neil would probably be off the phone and hopefully

Suky would be back so I could give her the letter. I could still make it home by seven thirty as long as I ran all the way.

"When's your mum going to be back, Arch?"

We were on our way upstairs and Archie put his finger on his lips to tell me to talk more quietly. "Any time now," he whispered. "And you've got to shush because Maisie's asleep already. Dad says it's the hot weather."

Then I heard footsteps in the hall and looked down to see Neil going from the lounge to the kitchen.

"Hi, Neil," I called down, in a bit of an excited voice. "I did it in fourteen minutes thirty-two! That's under fifteen! Did you hear the bell?"

Neil was flapping his arms around a bit and talking in a hoarse sort of whisper. "Keep your voice down, Billie. Maisie's asleep."

So I ran downstairs and said it again.

"Oh right... Well done... That's great..." But he wasn't concentrating properly. In fact he was looking over my shoulder through the hall window.

"Where's Gorky?"

"He was in the drive a minute ago."

Neil went out of the front door, but I shot past him. This was something helpful I could do.

"It's okay, Neil. I'll go down the drive and check he's there. Don't worry."

But when I'd run over the pebbly bit and could see right down to the bottom of the drive, I froze.

Both gates were open. And at that very second Neil called out from the front door, "You *did* shut the gate, didn't you, Billie?"

My mind raced back to the moment I'd rushed through the gate and bashed it against the wall. I'd been so busy checking my watch that I'd not made sure the gate had swung back, even though I know it has to be closed because of Gorky.

My stomach squeezed in fear.

A second later Suky's car swung in, fast. She didn't get out and shut the big gate, like she normally does, just zoomed straight up to the pebbly bit at the top of the drive. I saw her face when she passed me – all tight and white. That gave me a horrible feeling.

Please don't let anything have happened to Gorky.

I walked back across the pebbles with heavy footsteps. Suky, Neil and Archie were gathered round the car. Neil was reaching into the back seat and Archie was trying to see over his shoulder. As I got nearer I heard Neil say, "Billie must have left the gate open," and then Suky's words made my legs too heavy to take another single step. "That stupid girl!"

All the blood seemed to drain from my face. *Please don't let anything have happened to Gorky. Please don't let anything have happened to Gorky.* And right in the middle of my world collapsing around me, there was banging on an upstairs window, and everyone looked up to see Maisie with tears dripping down her face. She must have woken up with all the commotion and been wondering what was happening.

"Keep Gorky in the car," Neil said to Suky, taking charge. "I'll drive him straight to the vet's. You go and phone to warn them that we're on our way."

"I feel so terrible," said Suky in a shaky voice. "I could have killed him."

He's not dead. At least he's not dead.

Neil put his arm round her shoulder. "It wasn't your fault, darling. He just came straight out in front of your car."

It's my fault. I left the people gate open. All my fault.

"Do you think he's broken any bones?" That was Archie.

"I don't know. I think he's just a bit bruised and battered," said Neil, getting in the car.

Suky turned to go back into the house but I had to speak to her straight away, even though the heaviness had reached my mouth now and I wasn't sure if it would work properly. "Sorry, Suky. I thought the gate had swung back, you see... Sorry."

She turned round and took a deep breath before she looked at me, then tried to smile, but it didn't work because it never reached her eyes. "Don't worry, Billie. I think he'll be all right."

Maisie was banging hard on the window now, calling out, "Come up here, Mummy!"

So Suky hurried inside and Archie followed. I wasn't sure whether she wanted me in her house now or whether it would be best to just say bye and go back home. But I hadn't even given her the letter...

My hand went to my pocket and my insides seemed to shrink. The letter wasn't there.

12 The Truth?

When Neil had driven off, Archie asked me if I wanted to go on the computer. His face was a bit white, and that made me feel so bad that I couldn't even answer him. My brain was all clogged up with terrible thoughts about how I could have killed poor Gorky. I should have thought when I got to the gate and not gone rushing on just to show Neil how fast I was. I'd only just promised myself to think harder before I did things, and then I'd gone and broken my promise straight away.

"Gorky'll be okay, don't worry, Billie," Archie said as we went back into the house.

He was trying to make me feel better, but nothing

could make me feel better at this moment. Too many bad things had happened.

"Hello, Billie."

I looked up. Maisie was sitting on the top stair with her thumb in her mouth and her other hand clutching the old raggedy kangaroo that's her cuddler. Her face was a bit blotchy.

Suky came out of the kitchen looking worried, holding the phone. She went straight to the bottom of the stairs and spoke to Maisie without even looking at me and Archie.

"Mummy's just making a quick phone call, darling, then she'll come and tuck you up, all right?"

Maisie didn't answer. She was too busy staring at me with droopy, sleepy eyes. "Jenny did the rest of my hair when you'd finished *your* bit, Billie."

I don't know how I didn't gasp out loud. I couldn't believe that she'd come out with it, just like that! I hadn't thought that things could possibly get any worse in my life, but they just had, with those words of Maisie's. I whipped my head round to check that Suky had gone back into the kitchen. Thank goodness, she had. But the door was open.

I put my finger on my lips, frowned at Maisie and shook my head.

"I didn't tell Mummy it was you," she said without taking her thumb out of her mouth.

"Ssh!" I said to her, trying to smile. But it was no good standing there. I had to get away. Before Suky came back.

"I've got to go now," I told Archie.

"Don't you want a go on the computer?"

"No, I told Mum I'd go straight back home."

So Archie went upstairs, and I was nearly out of the front door when Suky's voice made me swing round.

"Billie, am I to understand that *you* were the one who cut Maisie's hair the other day?" Her eyes were flashing.

I gulped.

Truth or lie? Truth or lie? Think, Billie. Think.

If I told the truth the whole parent plan would be ruined. But if I told a lie, would Suky believe *me* or Maisie? Perhaps she believed Maisie already. Maybe she just wanted me to admit it. Grown-ups often do things like that – to catch you out. Yes, the truth would be better, as long as I wrapped it up with great big enormous sorries.

"I'm really, really, really, *really* sorry, Suky. You see, I thought—"

Her voice was hard and sharp. "I'm afraid I'm not in the mood for hearing what you thought, Billie. In fact, I think I'd better phone your mum and tell her to come and pick you up..."

My eyes flew open with alarm, but I had to pretend there was nothing wrong. "It's okay, you don't have to tell her. I came here on my own 'cos I'm allowed, now I'm just about eleven."

She raised her eyebrows, but the rest of her face had no expression. My mouth was dry. My shrunken inside organs were wobbling about. If Suky found out that *this* was a lie too...

"Bye then...Suky... And sorry...about everything..."

She said bye but went straight off to get Maisie, so I let myself out and set off down the drive with my head down and my hands in my pockets, and that got me wondering what had happened to my letter. I must have dropped it on my way over here. Probably when I had to go flat against the hedge because of the fast car. It was really important that I found it again before someone else did.

My whole body felt floppy and full up of pounce thoughts and I stopped halfway down the drive to kick a stone hard. Everything had gone wrong. I'd made Gorky get injured. Suky hated me. Neil probably did too. Even Maisie had dobbed on me. And now I wasn't sure if Archie ought to get the flowers at all. Flowers as a "sorry" present weren't really the same as flowers for no reason.

I went out of the gate and walked slowly along on the same side of the road that I'd come on, searching the ground all around. I was just thinking about Gorky wandering into the road without looking right or left because of only being a dog and not knowing the Green Cross Code, when I jumped about a mile into the air because of a massive thunderclap. The sky had gone dark purply-grey, but my eyes had been on the ground so I hadn't even noticed. It was about to bucket down any minute and I was going to get soaked. I looked at my watch. Twenty-seven minutes past seven. So now I was in for a telling-off for being late home as well. My throat was suddenly hurting too much even to walk so I stopped. Then my eyes started to water, and actual tears came out. I haven't cried since Year Four when I trapped my finger in the car door.

My head was getting wet because of the rain that was falling in big slow drops. I was going to be soaked right through by the time I got home. Maybe Mum would feel sorry for me when she saw me. I could say I was late because I'd stopped to shelter for a while, but then decided to keep going, even though I'd get soaked, to save her from worrying.

So I started walking again and after about ten minutes I was totally sopping wet. The backs of my legs felt sticky with the dirt that was splashing up. Then I got another spraying when a red car went past really close to me. A bit further up the road the car pulled over. I felt sick. This was the main reason why Mum didn't want me coming out here on my own, you see. Because of *stranger danger*.

The car window wound down, and a head appeared.

"Let me give you a lift. You're getting soaked."

I recognized that voice. Jenny, the hairdresser,

was smiling at me through the spikes of rain. She must have seen me hesitating, but it was only because if I had a lift I wouldn't be able to keep on looking for my letter.

"Come on. Hop in, Billie!"

Jenny seemed like a nice person, and I liked the thought of the warm cosy car, so I got in quickly.

"Clunk click!"

She meant me to do my seat belt up. That's what Mum always says.

When we pulled away I looked sideways at her and saw she was still smiling. Chuckling, in fact.

"You youngsters don't bother with coats and things these days, do you?"

I wasn't sure what to say and I could feel myself going a bit red, because although she wasn't exactly asking me what I was doing out in the rain, I felt as though that was what she really wanted to know. I said I'd been out training, but it had started raining, and then we both laughed because of the rhyme, and I started hoping that if she ever told Mum that she'd picked me up, she wouldn't say where, she'd just say that I was out training.

"Erm, you don't need to take me all the way, Jenny. It's nearly stopped raining now."

"Don't be silly. I've got to go past your place to get home. I'll drop you outside."

Oh no.

Now I just had to pray that Mum wasn't looking out of any windows ready to pounce the moment she saw me.

The very second Jenny pulled the handbrake on I jumped out of the car. "Thank-you-very-much-for-the-lift-bye-bye," I gabbled then shot up the path.

I got a bit wetter as I went round the back and let myself into the kitchen. Mum had the phone to her ear, but she let it drop to her side when she saw me. Her face was all pinched. "Oh there you are! I was getting worried. It's pouring down! Why didn't you come home? I was just trying to get through to Suky to check you'd not done anything stupid like go round to her place." I gulped. "But now you're here, I don't need to bother."

She put the phone down, and I tried not to let my big sigh of relief show.

"Sorry, Mum… You see, I went a bit further than I

meant to, and then I took shelter for ages but the rain didn't stop so I decided to make a run for it in the end. I knew you'd be worried, you see."

"Well go and take your wet clothes off. You're dripping all over the floor."

I passed Victoria in the hall, rushing into the kitchen. "Hi, sweetie! What a sight!" Then I heard her telling Mum that she'd just tried on her new trousers, and they were only pinching a bit now.

"That's great, Tigs!" said Mum in an excited squeak.

I didn't know what was so great about it. Anyone'd think Victoria had won the lottery, the way Mum was acting all happy. Huh! She never used that voice with me these days.

"Now what did I come in here for in the first place?" Victoria was saying. "Oh yes, have my jogging bottoms been washed yet? I left a pound coin in the pocket."

I froze on the second stair.

"You're in luck – I've not put the wash on yet."

There was a silence while I guessed Victoria was fishing around in the washing machine.

"That's funny! I know I left it in this pocket. It's for the locker. I always keep it in the zip bit, only I usually remember to transfer it to my other bottoms when one pair goes in the wash."

I could hear the sound of coins rattling around. Mum was looking in her purse. "Don't worry, Tigs... I've got a couple of pound coins in here... Hang on." My heart started lurching around. "That's funny... I definitely had two..."

"It's okay, Emma, I'll borrow one off someone."

"No, no... Take this one, but I just don't understand..."

Her voice faded out, and I knew Victoria would be coming out any second so I ran upstairs two at a time.

Next thing I heard was Mum calling out to Quentin to "Come here a mo", and something told me this was going to be terrible.

I hate going to bed early, especially when it's still light, but it seemed like the only way to avoid a big interrogation, so I got into my nightie and dived under the duvet. It was completely dark under there, even with my eyes open, and my thought bubble was dark as well because my parent plan was in ruins, and now I was in trouble at home as well.

I never realized how dark darkness could be.

13 The Court Case

I lay awake for ages that night, and when Mum came in to see me I pretended to be asleep so she couldn't start quizzing me about the missing money. She didn't try to wake me up, thank goodness. Just crept out. She was cross though. I could feel it. Even through the bedclothes. When she'd gone I started wondering what I was going to say in the morning when she mentioned it. It really depended on whether Quentin had noticed some of his money was missing. There'd been so many coins on the chest of drawers I didn't see how he could possibly have known the exact amount. But if he *did* know, I was in big trouble. It'd be obvious I must be the guilty one if all *three* of them found out that they'd lost some money, and I'd just have to own up.

I crept along to the bathroom feeling like a little mouse wishing it could hide from the big monster cat, but knowing that the cat will get it in the end. Then I stopped in my tracks at the sound of Mum's voice. She was talking to Quentin in their bedroom. Her voice was scarcely more than a whisper.

"What about your change on the chest of drawers? Did you check that?"

"Uh-huh."

My eyes flew open. So Quentin hadn't noticed. Perhaps I was saved after all. Did I dare to lie about the rest of the missing money?

But as it happened I didn't have to say a word because Granny Caroline phoned at breakfast time, and Mum was on the phone for so long that afterwards she had to rush around like mad, so there wasn't time to think about missing money.

I had another horrible day at school, though. Liam kept waiting till Archie wasn't around then saying nasty things about Quentin and Victoria. I just ignored him, but I wasn't ignoring him on the inside. That bit was hurting. All I could think was: *Never mind, Billie, it'll soon be the summer holidays.* There was only one more week then we'd be breaking up, and although I knew there was no chance of Liam magically changing into a nice person over the holidays, at least there'd be loads of people from other schools when we got to secondary in September, so he might find someone new to pick on.

Meanwhile I'd got a whole six and a half weeks to get my parent plan going again. It would need some serious work, but I was sure I could do it if I really tried hard. I mean, I'd admitted to Suky about cutting Maisie's hair, so now she knew I was an honest person. That was one good thing. Also Archie had promised me that Gorky definitely wasn't going to die, so all I had to do was wait for him to get home from the vet's, then I'd use my next two weeks' pocket money on a present for him, like a nice ball that I could throw for him to run and bring back to me. And I'd make sure I spent as much time as possible at Archie's all through the holidays and do loads of helpful things, and running things with Neil too.

I'd decided not to bother about looking for my letter because the wind would probably have blown it right under a hedge. And the rain would have soaked it and made it go rotten by now. It didn't really matter anyway because I could remember roughly what was in it so I'd just do another one. It wouldn't take a minute. I'd discovered that Mrs. Palmer was completely wrong about how you shouldn't rush and you're supposed to dig deep into your brain to find the best possible words. Writing stuff down is easy. You just write what you're thinking. I proved that with my last letter.

So all in all things weren't half as bad as I'd thought.

"You! Sit! Now!"

Mum was furious. Her face was white, with little red bits at the tops of her cheeks, and her lips were quivering. My mind was whizzing round like a washing machine. Was it because of the money? Had Suky told her about Maisie? Or worse, Gorky?

"I bumped into Jenny Grover today, and she told me she picked you up in the pouring rain last night. I don't know how I managed not to explode when she said you were jogging along on those dangerous bends on the road to Archie's…"

Mum paused. I wasn't sure if I was supposed to speak, but I couldn't think of a single thing to say, and anyway there wasn't enough spit in my mouth for talking. So I just sat there.

"…I phoned Suky and she confirmed that you were at her house yesterday evening…"

My heart was sinking down through the floorboards.

I felt as though I was in court and Mum was the lawyer. Her voice was getting louder with every word she spoke.

"…and it appears you told her you were *allowed* to go round there! I can't believe you lied so blatantly…"

Quentin came in the room at that moment, but went straight out again when he saw the court case going on. Mum folded her arms fiercely and her neck came forward like a terrible giant tortoise. As soon as she started up again I knew we were coming to the most horrible bit.

"And naturally I felt curious as to why you should suddenly take it into your head to go round to Archie's... So I asked Suky if she could throw any light on the subject, and she couldn't, except to say that she'd noticed five pounds in change under Archie's bed when she was cleaning his room this morning, and she wondered if it could possibly have anything to do with *that*?"

Mum stood there fuming and shaking, and I sat there silent and still and sinking.

"Well? What have you got to say? Could the money under Archie's bed by any chance have anything to do with the money that's missing from my purse and Victoria's jogging bottoms? Hmm?"

Her eyes were big and accusing. I sucked my cheeks in to try and get some spit in my mouth so I could say something.

"I owed Archie the money, you see..." I began, watching her face closely. Her expression didn't change at all. "...because of a kind of bet..." The muscles in her jaw went a bit saggy and she sat down.

"Go on."

But I didn't dare risk any more. "I know you're not supposed to bet. I won't...do it again."

She put her elbow on the table and rested her head in her hand. "Is that all?"

My brain started doing cartwheels trying to work out what she meant, or if she was setting me one of those grown-up traps. Maybe she was giving me one last chance to tell the truth before she flew off into a red-hot rage again. I nodded and licked my lips because the dryness from my mouth was spreading.

She spoke very quietly, as though she was completely worn out from the last lot of talking. "Suky said there was five pounds in change under Archie's bed. Well I've worked out that there's one pound fifty missing from my purse, and Tigs has lost a pound." Her eyes bored into mine. "I want to know, is that *all* the money you took from this house, Billie?"

Truth or lie? Truth or lie?

Quentin says he hasn't lost any so a lie would be safe.

But then something flashed into my mind.

Something really obvious. And this was it... I could get the money back from Archie. "I'll pay you and Victoria back, Mum. Honestly."

"It's nothing to do with the money. If you'd told the truth and asked us for a bit of money we might have felt like giving it to you – or at least lending it." Her anger was coming back. Perhaps I shouldn't have said anything. "It's the fact that you stole it and then told an elaborate lie about going jogging and stopping and sheltering and goodness knows what else." Her voice was getting louder and crosser. "You're grounded for the weekend, Billie, and you can forget about pocket money for the next month! Understand?"

Then she got up and went out and I was left there, feeling like a crumpled bit of wrapping paper that someone had chucked on the floor.

14 The Match Trick

It's Saturday afternoon, and I'm in the back garden weeding for Mum. The worst of her crossness has worn off, but she's still really upset about me taking the money, and she's hardly talked to me at all in the last twenty-four hours. She just walks round with a scowly, worn-out face as though I've exhausted her with my bad behaviour.

It's my birthday on Monday. I can't imagine that anyone's bought me a present, because they all seem to hate me. Well, Quentin's just acting normally, but then he only ever does things in a boring, normal kind of way. Victoria did try to talk to me about the money and everything, so I just said I was sorry. What else could I say? She doesn't hug me as much as she used to, or call me sweetie and darling, and I can tell she's totally on Mum's side because she folds her arms and stands close to Mum when I'm in the room. They ought to buy themselves T-shirts that say *I HATE BILLIE.*

"Have you seen this?"

Quentin was sitting on the back-door step and beckoning me to come over. I didn't really want to. I feel guilty when I'm anywhere near Quentin. I keep reminding myself that he doesn't know I took his money, but it doesn't make it any better. In fact it makes it worse. And then there's that thing I said on Pudding Hill about him not being any kind of a dad. Even though I don't want Quentin round here I still can't bear thinking about that. It sets off a rushing noise inside my head, and I feel like blocking my ears to make it go away.

He patted the step and I sat down. He was holding a box of matches, and he took one out and lit it. I couldn't work out what he was doing. Mum was giving us both a disapproving look through the kitchen window. Her lips were pursed so tight anyone'd think she'd been sucking lemons. Quentin obviously didn't realize he wasn't supposed to be talking to me, and he definitely shouldn't be *doing* stuff with me. He was supposed to be ignoring me like everyone else was.

"Watch carefully."

I did as I was told because it was less boring than weeding. I had to squash up a bit to fit on the doorstep, but it would only be for a minute. When the match had almost burned right down, he blew it out really gently so it was totally bent and black and flaky.

"See this?"

He was holding the very end of the match between his thumb and the next-door finger. There wasn't anything to see yet but I watched closely. With his other hand he seemed to be winding something like a really fine thread very slowly round and round the match, only I couldn't see a thread. I leaned forwards and concentrated hard. A second later he jerked hard on the thread, and the end of the match shot off.

"That's amazing!" I was staring at the little charred end of the match that lay on the ground, then I looked at Quentin. His face was perfectly serious, but a second later he suddenly cracked up laughing, and I felt a bit stupid because the whole thing had been a trick after all. "How did you do that? I don't get it."

"Works every time!" he spluttered. "Look… I'll show you again…"

This time I squashed up even more closely and stared without blinking so I wouldn't miss a thing. There definitely wasn't any thread, but I still didn't get how he made the end of the match fall off, even though I was right up close. So he did it again and explained about flicking it off with his finger and thumb.

"Oh, I get it!" I said slowly. "That's quite good, that is. Can I have a go?"

I thought he might say something stupid about me being too young to play with matches, but he just handed me the matches, and when I lit one he showed me how to tilt it to make sure it didn't burn out too soon or burn down too fast. Then I took hold of the imaginary thread.

"That's right… Take your time… Wind it round… Slowly does it… And flick!"

I did exactly what he said and it worked perfectly.

"Hey, I did it! Can I have another go?"

But Mum suddenly opened the kitchen window and spoke snappily. "I thought you were supposed to be weeding, Billie."

"She's just taking a break," said Quentin.

Mum nodded, and I saw a puzzled look go across her face. She didn't shut the window, and I think she wanted to listen to what we were saying in case Quentin was breaking the rules and being nice to me. *Was* Quentin being nice to me? Well...yes, actually. He was.

When I had that thought, it felt like a pounce thought only ten times worse because I didn't want him to be nice to me after what I'd called out on Pudding Hill. I wished I could block my ears, shake my head and close my eyes to stop myself from being able to hear those horrible words of mine. I tried to put some sentences together in my head that I might be able to say to him to show I didn't exactly hate him or anything, it was just that he wasn't the right kind of person to be my dad, but the words were like drops of oil in a big patch of water. They just kept blobbing about on their own and wouldn't stick together.

I was staring at the lawn. "Archie's dad made daisy chains with Archie's little sister," I blurted out. It wasn't anything to do with what I really want to say, but at least it was something.

"I bet she enjoyed that."

"Yeah…he's nice, Archie's dad."

"Lucky Archie."

"Yeah. And he's a good runner – Archie's dad, not Archie."

"Yes, your mum said."

"He thinks I'm a good runner too."

I frowned and thought about what I'd just said. *Did he? Had Neil ever actually said that he thought I was a good runner?*

"I'm not surprised, you *are* a good runner!"

I flicked my head round to look at Quentin, surprised.

"How do *you* know?"

"Well I saw you running up Pudding Hill for a start. That was pretty nifty!"

"We could buy a stopwatch and you could time me!"

What did I say that for? It's Neil who's going to time me, isn't it?

"Good idea."

"Can I have one…? For my birthday, I mean."

It suddenly seemed like the most important thing in the world to have a stopwatch as soon as possible. I found myself gripping Quentin's elbow and fixing him with a really urgent look. "They're not expensive, are they?"

"About two pounds fifty, I think," Quentin said, looking right back into my eyes.

Two pounds fifty. Wham! The words hit the air like a big boulder hitting the middle of a lake. I couldn't turn away from Quentin however much I wanted. Something was stopping me. So there we were, face to face with the dreaded words rippling off fainter and fainter all over the garden. I took my hand off his elbow, feeling embarrassed that I'd been clutching him like that, and he raised his eyebrows just a tiny bit, like you do when you're waiting for someone to answer you. But his eyes weren't waiting for the answer, because his eyes already knew the answer. I'd realized that as soon as he'd spoken. Quentin knew I'd taken that money of his. He'd always known. So why hadn't he said so when Mum asked him? Why would Quentin want to get me out of trouble? That was the only question that I couldn't answer.

"Let's wait and see what happens on Monday, shall we?" he said with a small smile, as he got up and turned to go into the house.

But all of a sudden I didn't want him to go. He might know some more tricks...or even if he didn't...I just wanted him to stay out here a bit longer. "Sh...shall we make another spear?"

"I've got to see a man about a dog, I'm afraid."

"A dog? Are we getting a dog?"

He chuckled as he went inside. "It's a saying. It just means I've got to go out."

I stood up feeling a bit funny and watched him go. He turned and gave me a really nice smile. "I won't be long."

Then the phone rang so I couldn't ask him exactly *how* long.

"Oh hello, Suky!" Mum's voice came through the window. "How are you? And how's Gorky getting on now?"

Suky! Oh no!

When I'd recovered from the shock I dived across the lawn and picked up the trowel. Suddenly weeding seemed like the best thing to be doing. It would be harder for Mum to go mad at me if I was helping her. My brain was back in whirling washing-machine mode. I was still full of Quentin thoughts, but now there were other bigger thoughts joining in. Mum knew about Gorky after all. This was terrible. Why hadn't she said anything to me about him?

I stuck in the trowel; I yanked out the weeds. I weeded harder than a professional weeder breaking the world weeding record. And all the time my brain tried to imagine what Suky could be saying that went on and on for so long, and just made Mum come out with slow thoughtful yeses, like she was following a story.

After about a minute the yeses stopped, and Mum spoke in a low, embarrassed voice. My whole body was completely still so I could listen my hardest.

"Well, she's grounded for the weekend actually… Oh, I see… Yes, I suppose that would be all right… Yes, that's right. It's on Monday."

Did she mean my birthday? What was that about then? I took a couple of steps nearer so I wouldn't miss a single word, but the rest was just Mum saying "Bye" and "See you soon".

I shot back to the flowerbed because Mum was coming out.

"That was Suky."

I didn't look up in case I was red.

"She was telling me about poor old Gorky."

I still didn't look up.

"They had to take him to the vet's because Suky ran into him in the drive by mistake…"

I froze.

"Don't look so shocked, he didn't break any bones, just got slightly winded and a bit bruised… But anyway, when the vet examined him it turned out that Gorky had swallowed a cork, and they had to take it out as soon as possible or he might have died, so it was a good job Suky *did* run into him!"

I stood up slowly with my mouth hanging open, while Mum looked into the distance. "You know I sometimes think things like that are fate."

She'd never said anything like that to me before.

It was as though she thought I was a grown-up. It felt nice.

"I agree," I said slowly. "Because...fate's like a coincidence, only bigger, isn't it?"

Mum stopped looking into the distance and fixed me with a strong expression in her eyes. "Yes... Yes, that's a good way of putting it." Then she gave me a hug, which I hadn't been expecting. She felt soft and warm. "Suky's bringing Archie round. They've got you a birthday present, but Suky didn't want Archie taking it to school on Monday in case anything happened to it, so they'll be round in a few minutes."

Mum went back into the house after that, and I finished off the weeding. But something had changed. I didn't know what, and I didn't know why. I didn't even know *where* the change was. I mean was it in Mum or Quentin? Was it in the earth or in the air? Or was it inside me?

15 The Big Surprise

I was in my room when Suky's car drew up. I saw it through the window, but I didn't go down. It was too embarrassing and scary. The last time I'd seen her she'd hardly said bye to me, she'd been so cross. Archie was clutching something wrapped up in silver paper. Even the thought of my birthday present didn't make me feel any better. It might all be a massive trick for Suky to get over here so she could tell Mum in person all the bad things about me. I shivered even though I was hot.

"Billie! They're here!" Mum was calling me down. I'd have to go.

In the kitchen I said hello, but I didn't look at Suky. It was too embarrassing. Archie handed me the present straight away.

"Hey thanks, Arch."

"Oooh, a prezzie!" said Victoria coming in at that moment. "Let's see what it is, Billie."

I ripped off the silver paper and found a lovely big hardback notebook inside. The cover was padded like a cushion in dark green and light green with yellow flowers, and the pages of the book looked so clean and white and felt so smooth.

"Hey thanks!" I said again, but this time I looked at Suky properly, and even though I wasn't expecting a smile she gave me a really nice big one. "I can write down all my..." But I stopped. How could I explain about the stuff inside my head?

"Your thoughts and ideas," Archie finished off for me.

"Yes," I said. "I'll put a label across the front that says *Billie's Book of Important Thoughts and Ideas*. That's what I'll do."

I saw Mum and Suky exchange a look, then Suky said, "Perhaps you're going to be an author when you grow up, Billie."

I did a sort of shrug and said, "Or a runner."

"Yes, I know you're a good runner..."

But then there was an embarrassing silence because the mums were probably both thinking about the time I ran over to Archie's.

Victoria broke the silence in her brightest voice. "Anyway, how are you, Archie? I haven't seen you for ages."

"All right, thanks," said Archie.

"Well, do sit down everyone," said Mum. "I'll put the kettle on. Billie's been gardening for me."

"Ooh! Let's have a look," said Suky. "Come on, Billie. Give me a guided tour!"

She seemed to be completely back to normal. Not cross or anything. Archie was glued to one of Quentin's magazines, so I went outside with Suky. It was funny because I'd only just been out here with Quentin, and before I knew it I was in a thought bubble, imagining Suky doing the match trick. It wouldn't have been right. She didn't really suit match tricks.

"This is the bit I've been weeding." I pointed to it, but I wasn't sure what else to say.

Suky didn't seem so interested now. She cleared

her throat. "Billie…" *Uh-oh…* "I just wanted to tell you not to worry about that Gorky business. Did your mum explain that it turned out to be a good job we *did* take him to the vet's?"

There was quite a lot of soil in the grass where I'd shaken it off the weeds. I started kicking it back on to the flowerbed so I didn't have to look at her. "Yeah."

I knew I should have been thanking her for pretending it happened in the drive so Mum didn't know it had been my fault. But I didn't know what to say.

"And also, Archie mentioned that you were trying to save me time by cutting Maisie's hair… I hadn't actually realized that…"

I kept my eyes on the soil. "Yes."

Suky was saying nice things to try and make everything better, and I should have been answering her properly, but I didn't even feel like talking now.

"And Billie…" Out of the corner of my eye I could see that she was pulling something out of the zipped-up bit of her combats. I turned my head to look at it properly, and my stomach squeezed up tight. It was my letter. All crumpled and dirty, but definitely my letter. *TO SUKY FROM BILLIE.*

I stared at it and tried to think what to say, but no words would come into my head. I was completely embarrassed now and just wished I could get the letter back. And no way did I feel like talking to Suky about the parent plan either, only I wasn't sure why not when I'd been so desperate before. I thought it might be to do with the way she looked. She just didn't seem very motherly in her tight white top and with her toenails painted blue. I imagined her hugging me, and I didn't think she'd be as soft and warm as Mum because of her thinness. And yet I used to like the way Suky looked. So what had changed? I didn't get myself.

She coughed. "I...er...found this at the side of the road when I got out of the car to pick up poor old Gorky. I put it in my jacket pocket and forgot about it with all the drama, but then I found it today."

My heart was hammering. I was really kicking that soil out of the grass now.

She carried on in a rush. "I didn't open it, though, because I wasn't sure if it was for me. I mean, I thought it was more likely to be for someone at *school* called Suky…"

I jerked my head round. She'd given me the perfect words to say.

"Yes, it was! It was for Suky…at school. That's who it was for. I'll give it her on Monday."

She handed it to me, and I stuffed it as deep into my jeans pocket as it would go.

"Good," she said. "That's that sorted out, then!"

I knew I was a bit red, and I was desperate for this conversation to end because it was too jerky and embarrassing.

"You've made a very good job of this bed, Billie! Well done, you!"

I nodded like a robot that had nearly run out of battery. Then Archie came out to find me, thank goodness.

"Let's go up to your room, Billie."

Suky went in to find Mum, and we two went upstairs. What a relief.

In the hall we passed Quentin's spear. Mum had left it on the little table, and Archie picked it up. "Hey, this is good. Who made this?"

"Er...Quentin..."

"Oh right, this is the spear you were talking about. Cool! Shall we fly it? Does it work? It looks wicked."

That robot-running-out-of-battery feeling hadn't gone away, so my voice came out a bit flat. "It needs a bigger place than our garden."

"Oh yeah, you went to Pudding Hill last time, didn't you? Let's ask if we can go there now. Come on."

"My mum won't let me, I know."

"Well, what time's Quentin going to be back?"

"I dunno... He might be ages. Anyway, if I'm allowed out, I'd rather come back to your place. We'd have a far better time there, honestly."

Archie wrinkled his nose. "What, better than flying a spear? I wish my dad could make something this good. He wouldn't have a clue, though. Let's ask Quentin to take us to Pudding Hill when he gets back."

I got a picture of Archie, Quentin and me all together on Pudding Hill, and Liam and his gang turning up and saying nasty things about Quentin. I frowned to myself, trying to think what Archie would say back. Probably nothing, because he'd be too busy having another go with the spear. But it was easy for Archie to ignore Liam. *He* didn't have to worry about having a really old stepdad, did he? Although Quentin didn't seem so bad now. Maybe because of the match trick. Or maybe... I didn't really know why. He just didn't.

"Go and ask your mum how long Quentin's going to be, Billie."

So I went downstairs on my robot legs. "Mum, when will Quentin be back?"

Her eyes darted from side to side, all secretive and silly. "You'll have to wait and see, won't you!"

I didn't get what was going on. "Can't you just tell me?"

"Any minute now I should think." Then she leaned forwards. "Honestly, Suky, Quentin's like a big kid at the moment!"

As I went back up to Archie I wondered what Mum was talking about because Quentin's nothing like a big kid.

"Hey, Billie! Look!" Archie was leaning out of my bedroom window.

"Is he back?"

"No, but why are our mums standing at the gate? What's going on?"

I went to have a look and got a nasty surprise because Liam, Josh and Tom were just down the road.

"Let's go and see what they're waiting for, Billie. Come on!"

And next minute Archie was racing downstairs. No way did I want to go out there, though. But then I heard a great roaring noise, and I couldn't resist leaning out to look down the road. Above the noise came the sound of Victoria's voice. "He's here! Daddeeeeeee!" She started jumping up and down, and so did Mum and Suky. Liam was staring at them, and then he looked up. It was too late for me to duck out of sight. He'd seen me.

"Daddeee!" he mimicked Victoria, and Josh and Tom fell about laughing.

But the roaring was getting louder now, and it made them stop laughing and look round to see what was making such a big noise. I followed their eyes and understood why they were so silent and still all of a sudden. There, coming round the bend, was a great big motorbike, all gold and black and shiny like a glowing spaceship.

Mum and Suky were clutching each other with excitement. Archie was yelling up at me to come down. Victoria had her shoulders hunched and her fists in her mouth like a little girl. The motorbike had stopped right outside our house. I could just about make out the words that gleamed in bright gold at the back of it...*HONDA GOLDWING*.

And there, on the enormous black seat, all in leathers and wearing a black space helmet, sat my stepdad, Quentin.

16 The Mean Machine

Everyone was crowding round the bike talking excitedly, but I couldn't hear a single word because Quentin hadn't switched the engine off and it was making quite a loud throbbing noise. I wished I was down there, only I couldn't make myself go because of Liam. I noticed that he'd taken a couple of steps forward, and I could tell he was dying to go even nearer, but the others were still by the hedge.

Where had the bike come from? I didn't get it. And what was Quentin doing riding it? Then I suddenly clicked about the magazines in our house. I'd got it all wrong thinking Quentin only *read* about motorbikes. He did actually ride them, after all.

And not any old motorbikes either, but a Honda Goldwing. It was amazing.

Mum turned round. "Come down, Billie!"

Her voice sounded extra loud because Quentin had switched off the engine and everything had gone suddenly quiet. That meant that everyone heard her so now they were all looking up at me. Even Quentin.

"Yes, come on, Billie!" said Victoria.

I looked over at Liam. He was still staring at the motorbike. It was obvious he thought it was brilliant. I bet he was wishing he could have a go on it.

"Come on!" Archie called up to me.

Then Quentin took his helmet off, and his eyes were all twinkly. "Want a ride, Billie?"

I looked at Mum and she nodded, smiling. It was amazing. I was sure she'd never have let me go on a motorbike before Quentin came to live with us. But he must have made her realize it was safe.

The feeling that came sweeping up from my feet zinged its way through my body and left a cloud of the brightest tingles in my head. Out of the corner of my eye I could tell that Liam was looking up at me, but I didn't bother to look back. It was as though those bright tingles were making me strong.

I gave Quentin a big smile and nodded hard.

Huh! I'm not scared of you, *Liam Compton.*

"Come on, then!" Quentin pulled something out from behind him, and I saw that it was another helmet, only a bit smaller than his. He waved it up at me. "We got it specially!"

My heart swelled up, pushing everything out as though it needed more room. I couldn't help looking at Liam then, but when our eyes met he quickly looked down. The magic tingles were really working. I raced out of my room, down the stairs, out of the front door and right up to Quentin.

"Isn't it a nice surprise, Billie?" said Victoria, putting her arm round me.

I just nodded hard again.

"Daddy's been saving up for ages, you know, Billie. You see, he used to have a fantastic bike when we lived in Somerset, but he sold it when we moved up here…"

Mum stood behind me and rested her hand on my shoulder. "Go on then, love."

I looked over at Liam. His eyes were still glued to the bike. They reminded me of Maisie's eyes when she'd been staring at the Coke, dying to drink it. And Quentin was handing me the helmet now.

"That's an early birthday present from your mum," he said. "It's no ordinary helmet, you know!"

I looked at Mum because I didn't get what was different about it.

"It's got a microphone in it, love," she said, grinning. "So you can talk to each other as you ride along! Quentin's has got a microphone in it too."

"Cool!" said Archie.

I gave Mum a big hug and Quentin switched the engine on. It was so noisy it felt like we were wrapped up in our own little world. But I didn't want to get on the bike yet. You see, it wasn't right inside my head, and I had to sort it out first.

"Quentin..."

"Yes."

"You know the spear..."

"Yes."

"Well, it was just as good as this bike, you know..."

He nodded slowly as though he understood a bit.

"…and…and so was the match trick," I went on.

He was looking at me with soft eyes now.

"I mean…I like all three things…equally." I wasn't sure if I was explaining it very well. "What I mean is…"

"It's all right, Billie. I do understand." And I could tell from his eyes that he did.

"Let's try these helmets out, eh?"

I put mine on in a bit of a daze and climbed on to the bike. It felt enormous. Then I wrapped my arms round Quentin's waist and laid my head against his back.

A second later we were zooming off. I could hear lots of cheering that made me smile, and I actually turned round and grinned at Liam. It was so funny seeing the jealous look on his face.

I hadn't expected the ride to be all that brilliant because I'd never been very interested in motorbikes. But it was magic. A trillion times better than a fairground ride. We roared past Pudding Hill, and I had the courage to sit up straight and look round a bit. We sped along roads I'd hardly ever been on before, and I never ever wanted this ride to end.

"Enjoying yourself?" Quentin's voice came through inside my helmet.

I giggled because it felt as though I was on the phone. "It's wicked!" I said. "And Liam's so jealous."

"Is that one of those boys from your class?"

"Yeah, he's got a gang." It felt all right talking like this. "Because he's stupid."

"You're right there!" said Quentin.

I didn't say anything else, just sat up straighter on the bike and smiled to myself as we accelerated.

When we got back, everyone was just as we'd left them, except for Liam, Josh and Tom, who were hanging around at the end of the road, trying to pretend they weren't interested in the bike. Good. I didn't want them interfering in our family time. Victoria was holding another helmet that she must have kept in her wardrobe or somewhere because I hadn't seen it when I was in her room. It had scratches on it and wasn't very shiny so I guess she'd had it for ages.

"My turn now? Yes?"

Quentin nodded. "Come on."

I could tell Victoria was completely used to riding on the back of bikes because she stretched her arms up high and called out "Yessss!" as they sped off, while Mum and Suky and Archie cheered like mad. I noticed that Liam and the others were wandering off, and I said, "Good riddance!" even though they couldn't possibly have heard me.

"Quite right!" said Mum, putting her arm round me.

I didn't even know she knew who Liam was. Maybe she just guessed, if Victoria or Quentin had told her about Pudding Hill. I was glad she knew anyway, and I put my arm round her waist. Then we stayed like that to wait for Quentin and Victoria to get back.

17 The Anniversary

Much later, when Archie and Suky had gone, I sat in my room and found myself staring at the wall, going back over all that had happened during the day, and I suddenly remembered the letter in my back pocket. I took it out and put it on the desk. I could feel my cheeks getting hot just looking at it.

TO SUKY FROM BILLIE

I ought to get rid of it. The parent plan wasn't so set in my mind any more. In fact it seemed a bit like something from a dream. Not a daydream. A proper dream. But whatever happened, I definitely wouldn't need the letter. That had been a stupid idea. I was about to put it in the bin, when I stopped dead. Something was different about the back of the envelope. Something to do with the piece of Sellotape across the flap. What was it? Then I realized. This was proper Sellotape – wide and shiny. Nothing like the scabby little bit I'd put on.

My knees went weak. Had Suky opened my letter after all? Was that what she came round for really? Then my stomach lurched like a yo-yo down to the floor and back up again. Is that what she was talking to Mum about on the phone for all that time?

No, it couldn't have been. There wouldn't have been enough time for the Gorky story *and* the stuff about my letter all in that one phone call, would there? And anyway Suky would never tell Mum that her only daughter wanted to be adopted by another family, would she? No, that would have been cruel.

Mum *had* looked sad earlier on, though, hadn't she?

Yes, but that was before the phone call.

My mind was going mad trying to work out what had really happened. In the end I knew there was no way of finding out without asking, and I didn't want to risk having to explain myself. But there was one thing I *could* do. I could go downstairs and try to explain to Mum and Quentin that I'd been through a bit of a funny time thinking I didn't want to live in this family any more, but I'd stopped thinking it now. Yes, I *had* stopped. I really had. And not just because of Quentin getting the Honda Goldwing, either.

I got up and ran out of my room, but then I heard a funny noise coming from Victoria's room so I listened at the top of the stairs for a few seconds. It sounded like someone was crying, but it couldn't be Victoria. She was a grown-up. I put my ear to the door and realized it *was* her. She was doing big sobby crying, which made me feel really sorry for her and wonder what ever could be the matter. It's quite scary hearing grown-ups cry and I thought I'd better go and get Mum, so I rushed off downstairs and tried the kitchen, but she wasn't there so then I tried the living room, and that was when I saw Mum outside with Quentin. They were standing with their backs to the open window. Quentin had his arm round Mum's shoulder. They'd probably gone to look at the sunset because they sometimes did that. The sky had a bright pinky orange ball in the middle of it with streaks and blotches of purple round the edges.

"Are you sure she wants to be on her own, Quentin? I can't bear to think of her all sad up in her room," Mum was saying.

"She needs to work it through for herself." Quentin's voice was firm. "That's how she deals with things."

Mum didn't reply, she just laid her head on Quentin's shoulder. They both stayed perfectly still, staring at the sunset. I turned and crept out and back upstairs.

I stood on the landing for ages, wondering what to do. Quentin had seemed very sure that Victoria would be able to sort things out for herself, but it didn't sound like she was doing very well. Perhaps I'd just knock. She could always tell me to go away if she wanted to. After all, that's what I did to her when I was upset. Well, I wasn't upset exactly – more angry really. I felt a bit guilty about that now. It would kind of serve me right if Victoria *did* tell me to go away.

In fact I rather hoped she would, then I wouldn't feel so bad about that other time.

So I knocked, and the crying stopped straight away. There was quite a bit of silence before she opened the door, then she just stood there smiling, pretending there was nothing the matter at all, even though her eyes were all swollen and there were red bits round them.

"Erm…I just wondered if you were okay," I said.

She did one of those shuddery breaths that you do when you've been crying, and opened the door wider. "I'm being silly, that's all."

I went in, but I didn't know what to say so I kept quiet, and she sat on the bed and patted it for me to sit next to her.

"This is the day…" she said in a shaky voice, "eight years ago…when my mum died."

A big gasp came out of me and my stomach seemed to turn over. My mind was racing away. Victoria's mum had died, and I didn't even know. I hadn't even bothered to find out what had happened to her mum. I'd thought that Quentin was divorced. And eight years ago…Victoria is eighteen now, so that meant she was ten. *She was ten!* That's the same age as me. Oh poor, poor Victoria. I squashed up a bit closer to her and leaned my head on her shoulder like I'd seen Mum do with Quentin. I couldn't speak though, because of the big lump in my throat.

"It's stupid, isn't it, crying like this, just because of a date?" she said in a soft voice.

I shook my head and managed to say "No" because it absolutely wasn't stupid. Then I thought I really must try to speak, and I remembered something that Mum had said when I was little.

"Crying's good for you. It washes all the bad things out of the inside of you."

Victoria pulled away from me suddenly, and I thought at first that I must have said something to make her even more upset, but then I saw that she was frowning and concentrating. "That's really good advice, Billie. I'd never looked at it like that."

I felt quite proud, but it wasn't fair pretending I'd thought of it myself. "Actually, Mum made it up. I think I was three when Granny Caroline gave me some fairy wings, you see, and I thought I'd be able to fly, so I climbed up on the very top of the climbing frame, spread my wings and jumped off it. But of course I fell to the ground and broke my wrist where I put my hand down first."

Victoria gasped. "It must have been agony," she said.

"I didn't cry until we got to the hospital. The nurse said no wonder I was crying, it must really hurt, but Mum told her that she thought I was crying because of not being able to fly. And Mum was right because she understood the way my brain worked."

Victoria's shoulders started shaking, and I thought she was crying again, but when I looked at her I saw that she was laughing. "You're so good for me, Billie! Fancy launching yourself off a climbing frame! See how much better you've made me feel! I ought to stop going over sad things so much and just remember the good times, shouldn't I?"

"*I* go over things all the time."

"Do you? I'm glad I'm not the only one." She went serious again when she said that and did another of those shuddery breaths.

"It makes you feel like your head's going to blow off, doesn't it?" I went on.

She nodded, and I saw a few tears trickle down her face. "Sorry," she said. "About crying, I mean. It's stupid."

"I don't mind if you keep crying," I said, so she wouldn't have to worry about that. Then I remembered how Quentin had said she deals with things by working through them on her own. "Shall I go, Victoria?"

"If you want to..."

"No, I don't *want* to...I just thought you might wish you were on your own."

"No, I'd like you to stay. You make me feel better."

I didn't really know why I made her feel better because I wasn't even saying funny things any more.

"Are you sure?"

For an answer she held my hand. It took me straight back to the time she'd held my hand at Mum and Quentin's wedding and I'd absolutely hated her doing that. But now...

...it was different.

I didn't mind at all.

18 The Bursting of the Bubble

I was having a brilliant birthday. Victoria had already given me a W.H. Smith voucher, but then she'd had to go out to her aerobics class so it was just me and Mum and Quentin sitting round the table. We'd had a delicious tea, cooked by Mum, and I'd just blown out eleven candles on my big chocolate cake all in one puff.

"I think it's time you opened my present," Quentin suddenly said. "I'm afraid I'm not much good at wrapping up!"

I didn't care about wrapping, I was just looking forward to seeing what was inside. And when I saw, my skin tingled.

"Yay! Cool!" My eyes went straight to Quentin, and he winked.

I winked back. It didn't seem so stupid now that we had a secret of our own.

"Now Quentin can time you," said Mum.

"Yes," I said, clutching the silver stopwatch tight. "Yes, you can, can't you?"

"I'm looking forward to that, Billie."

His eyes had a look in them that I'd seen recently, and I had to rack my brains to think where. When I remembered, it gave me a shock because it wasn't even a look I'd seen in real life. It was the proud look on Neil's face from one of my thought bubbles. But this *was* real life, only it was Quentin, not Neil. And I know this seems really weird, but actually I liked it miles better.

So all there was left to do now was to give Mum and Quentin the letter I'd written.

After I'd talked to Victoria two days before, I'd gone back in my room and suddenly remembered that I'd been just about to go down and try to explain about my funny adoption feelings, but then I'd forgotten all about it, because of Victoria. Since then

I'd changed my mind about explaining stuff though. It didn't seem enough to *say* it. I should be *writing* it. What was it Mrs. Palmer had said?

"Every time you write something down, it automatically becomes more important than just saying it."

So I'd sat down at my desk and written the letter.

And now my heart was pounding against my ribs because I was handing it to Mum. "I wrote this for you because I thought I'd think of better words if they were written down."

Mum and Quentin exchanged a puzzled look. "A letter? For us?" asked Mum, sounding all confused.

"Yes…you'll see…it kind of explains…stuff…"

I licked my finger and pressed it down on a cake crumb on my plate then put it in my mouth. There were quite a few more crumbs on the plate so I kept doing that all the time they were reading the letter.

Mum's voice came out a bit choky, and that's what made me stop eating the cake crumbs and look up. "Oh Billie…" She'd got big tears rolling down her face and her lips were wobbling.

Quentin drew his chair up closer to hers so he

could hold her hand, then he held his other hand out to me, and without even thinking I went round to him, but there wasn't a chair, and I knew I was eleven, but I didn't care, I sat on his lap. And that was the moment when my whole parent plan thought bubble came right out of my head and began to float out of the house and away into the distance. And I suddenly got a picture of Mum and Quentin looking out at the sunset with Mum's head resting on Quentin's shoulder, and my thought bubble was in the picture too, floating across the streaky bits of sky. Then just when it was right in front of the pinky-orange ball of sun, it burst into nothingness. And at that very moment my whole body seemed to relax, and I knew that everything was going to be all right after all.

It was inspirational!

Billie's Book of Important Thoughts and Ideas

1. Have you ever looked at the inside of a chocolate box? You know how all the chocolates have got their own little compartment which is exactly the right shape for them to fit into? Well, I know this is a bit of a funny idea, but try to imagine you're called Strawberry Cream, and you live in your own special little space with all the other chocolates around you in their own places.

Now imagine that you're miserable being Strawberry Cream, and you keep on wishing you were round Toffee Whirl or oblong Turkish Delight. And sometimes you get cross and upset because you know the nutty chocolates at the other end of the box are laughing at you for being right next to Cherry Fondant, and Nutty Nougat says the meanest things about Cherry.

Now pretend that one day you try to change into another place in the box. Well I can tell you now, you won't fit, because of every little space being exactly the right size and shape for the chocolate that belongs there. So there's not even any point <u>trying</u> to move. You may as well just try to like it better where you are. And you can say to yourself, "There's nothing wrong with Cherry Fondant. And anyway, why should I care what Nutty Nougat thinks? He's nutty!"

When I was ten I didn't understand about all that. I do now, though. And it's not just to do with chocolates.

2. Quentin and Mum told me some important news this morning. It's the best news ever. They've been working out their <u>own</u> parent plan, and the plan is to get me adopted so Quentin won't just be my stepdad any more, he'll be my real dad. It's the best, best, best plan in the whole wide world. That's why I wanted to write it down in this book.

3. My name won't be Billie Stubbs any more. It'll be...

Billie Crawford

Billie Crawford!

Billie
Crawford

Billie Crawford

Billie Crawford